W9-COM-783

WHEN WE WERE SISTERS is . . .

**Winner of the Carol Shields Prize for Fiction
and the 2023 Vulgar Geniuses Fiction Award,
longlisted for the Aspen Words Literary Prize,
the National Book Award for Fiction, and
The Center for Fiction's First Novel Prize,
and a finalist for The Caliba Golden Poppy
Award For Emerging Diverse Voices**

**Named a Best Book of 2022 by *Time*,
The New Yorker, *Vox*, *Bustle*, *Ms. Magazine*,
Autostraddle, *The Chicago Review of Books*,
and NPR!**

"[Fatimah] Asghar's debut novel, *When We Were Sisters*, channels their poetic sensibilities into a tender tale about three young siblings—Noreen, Aisha, and Kausar—and the ways in which they care for each other after their parents die. The siblings, taken in by their neglectful uncle, learn to lean on one another. Captured in Kausar's thoughtful voice, grief ebbs and flows alongside a tumultuous journey of adolescence. Longlisted for a National Book Award, this exquisite debut wrestles with gender, siblinghood, family, and what it means to be Muslim in America—all through the lens of love."   —*Time*

"Unique structural and formatting choices interspersed throughout the book break up the narrative with a poetic quality, which is no surprise given Fatimah Asghar's first work is a poetry collection.... [A] lyrical coming-of-age debut."
—*Zibby Mag*

"Haunting . . . a knife-sharp story of . . . self-discovery."
—*People*

"Threaded with vignettes and poetic interludes, the novel constantly morphs into the shape of . . . new families—whether with temporary 'aunties and uncles,' their sisters, their uncle in a tender moment, or their lovers. No structure, even among siblings, is fixed. Asghar wants to pivot away from prevailing orphan narratives in which ragtag siblings come together and form an 'ideal family.'"
—*The Cut*

"*When We Were Sisters* braids lyric and narrative vignettes into a tender, vivid, heart-aching story of three orphaned sisters and the world they create together, the great beauty and stunning pain of that belonging. The book follows Kausar, the youngest, from early childhood into adulthood, her voice captured at every age with a poet's ear for language. The characters are so thoughtfully rendered, so three-dimensional in their flesh and blood and bone and infinite complications, their twinned capacities for kindness and for cruelty."
—*Electric Literature*

"Asghar's prose urges us to embrace the complexities of family, race, obligation, dreaming, and grieving. Her characters are achingly human in ways that make life hard for the living and easier for the dead—they are layered, hurting, and doing what they deem to be their best." —*Autostraddle*

"Focusing on the lives of three orphaned Muslim American sisters, and told from the perspective of the youngest, Kausar, *When We Were Sisters* contends with themes of poverty, gender, and abuse. It is . . . difficult to put down. . . . Asghar blends poetry with their storytelling to layer the narrative with historical poignancy. . . . A much-needed shattering of domestic myths, complication of diaspora literature, and challenge to entrenched class assumptions."
—*Kajal Magazine*

"[Asghar] gorgeously weaves the themes of grief and community, along with queerness and love, into prose that is compulsively readable and heartwrenching at the same time. . . . Despite the excavation of painful realities for the trio of siblings, Asghar also fills it with scenes of playful teasing, caring and attempts to claw back childhood after the death of a parent." —WBEZ Chicago

"[Asghar's] debut lyrical novel, *When We Were Sisters*, explores sisterhood, orphaning, and alternate family building. . . . At the heart . . . is Fatimah's unique voice, insistence on creating alternate possibilities of identity, relationships and humanity then the ones that society would box us into, and a deep play and joy embedded in the craft."
—PEN America

"We expect a lot from novels written by poets: a heightened sensitivity to language, brevity, a sustained sense of theme or metaphor. How wonderful when a poet's novel actually delivers. Asghar's debut, about a trio of Pakistani orphans and the sacrifices they make (or don't) to stay together after the death of their father, is a 300-pager that you can't put down—a typographically experimental work that maintains its focus on the humanity of its characters."

—*Vulture*

"Not to be missed . . . an achingly lovely story of sisterhood, loss, violence, and redemption." —*Ms. Magazine*

"Asghar is an outstanding poet and it's no wonder their debut novel is equally beautiful. The book follows three Muslim sisters as they navigate the world and discover who they are. Asghar's lyrical writing sings on every page."

—*Debutiful*

"Compelling . . . sometimes lyrical, sometimes heartbreaking . . . skillfully crafted . . . a moving journey . . . An assured first novel explores the bonds and divides among three orphaned sisters."

—*Kirkus Reviews* (starred review)

"[An] elegant debut novel . . . Asghar's poetic sensibilities are on full display in the lyrical and oblique prose, and the frequent formal experimentation enlivens the text. The result is a creative telling of a tender coming-of-age tale."

—*Publishers Weekly*

"Pop culture will have us believe that all parentless pain must be channelised into greatness in a Potter world or a Gotham City. Asghar's triumph lies in completely reclaiming identities from any such stereotypical lens. . . . Asghar shows a distinctive aptitude for translating the unsaid in our lives into emotions the characters contend with. Yet, they do it with a lyrical vulnerability that truly captures the world view of the place and the age of their characters."

—*Vogue India*

"[A] heartrending and lyrical novel . . . stunning."

—*She Does The City*

"A beautifully written story of building new bonds through tragedy and grief."   —*Book Riot*

"Vignettes with dark but tender prose that form a striking picture of the sisters' daily lives . . . A debut in fiction perfect for poetry readers, this poignant coming-of-age tale examines a girlhood torn apart by loss."   —*Booklist*

"In this captivating, gorgeously written book, Asghar weaves a tale of sisters in the wake of unspeakable loss. Propulsively readable and experimental in form, this is an unflinching look at family, grief and reclamation—of self and other."

—HALA ALYAN, author of *Salt Houses*
and *The Arsonists' City*

BY FATIMAH ASGHAR

If They Come for Us

When We Were Sisters

WHEN
WE
WERE
SISTERS

WHEN WE WERE SISTERS

A Novel

FATIMAH ASGHAR

ONE WORLD
NEW YORK

2023 One World Trade Paperback Edition

Copyright © 2022 by Fatimah Asghar

All rights reserved.

Published in the United States by One World, an imprint of
Random House, a division of Penguin Random House LLC, New York.

Grateful acknowledgment is made to Northwestern University Press for
permission to reprint an excerpt from "Another Attempt at the Telling" from
The Shared World: Poems by Vievee Francis (Evanston, IL: TriQuarterly Books/
Northwestern University Press, 2023, p. 10), copyright © 2023 by Northwestern
University Press. Published 2023. All rights reserved. Used by permission.

ONE WORLD and colophon are registered trademarks of
Penguin Random House LLC.

Originally published in hardcover in the United States by
One World, an imprint of Random House, a division of
Penguin Random House LLC, in 2022.

LIBRARY OF CONGRESS CATALOGUING-IN-PUBLICATION DATA
Names: Asghar, Fatimah, author.
Title: When we were sisters: a novel / by Fatimah Asghar
Description: First edition. | New York: One World, [2022]
Identifiers: LCCN 2022004574 (print) | LCCN 2022004575 (ebook) |
ISBN 9780593133477 (trade paperback) | ISBN 9780593133484 (ebook)
Subjects: LCGFT: Novels.
Classification: LCC PS3601.S46 W48 2022 (print) |
LCC PS3601.S46 (ebook) | DDC 813/.6—dc23
LC record available at https://lccn.loc.gov/2022004574
LC ebook record available at https://lccn.loc.gov/2022004575

Printed in the United States of America on acid-free paper

oneworldlit.com

2 4 6 8 9 7 5 3 1

Book design by Jo Anne Metsch

for my parents

for ru & keke

& for myself

The secret to knowing the secret is to speak, but
    we too often tell
the stories of no matter and avoid the one story
    that does matter.

In truth, we are bound by one story, so you'd
    think by now
we'd tell it, at least to each other.

—VIEVEE FRANCIS

1995

In a city, a man dies and all the Aunties who Aunty the neighborhood reach towards their phones. Their brown fingers cradle porcelain, the news spreading fast and careless as a common cold. Ring! [   ] is dead. Ring! Inna lillahi wa inna ilayhi raji'un. Ring! How sad. Ring! Only a few years after his wife. Ring! And his daughters? Ring! Three of them, yes. Ring! Alive. Ring! Ya Allah. Ring! [   ] is dead.

A man dies in a city he was not born in. Murdered. In the street. (Inna lillahi wa inna ilayhi raji'un.) A man dies in a city he only lived in for a handful of years. (How lonely.) A man dies in a city that his children were born in, but a city that will never be theirs, in a country that will never be theirs, on land that will never be theirs. (Ya Allah.) A father dies and the city and his children keep on living, the lights twinkling from apartment building to apartment building. All around the city, breath flows easily. All around the man, breath slows to a stop. The sky, who sees everything, looks down at him. And the moon, who is full, shines her milky dress on his dead body, bedded by the cement street.

———

In a city, a man dies. In a suburb in a different state, the man's brother-in-law celebrates by adding an extension to his family's house. A new deck spills out into their backyard. The man's brother-in-law renovates the basement: old moldy carpet pulled up and Moroccan marble tiles put in its place. The brother-in-law pores over them at the Home Depot, comparing prices, how happy it will make his wife, white, who he married when he first came to America. *A gorra?* his mom asked, the brown women in his family looking at each other, confused. *She found Islam because of me!* he explained, exasperated, not understanding why people couldn't see how he was going to earn extra points to heaven, his love enough to make someone convert. *You went to America and fell out of love with us,* his mom sighed, dramatic, as usual.

But brown women were so plentiful. He knew he could have them. White women found every simple thing he did exciting. It opened him. The lota in the bathroom, a marvel. Basic fruit chaat, the spiciest thing they'd ever tasted. How interesting he could become. *A gorra?* his cousins in Pakistan echoed in disbelief, some whispering *mashallah* as others turned away from him. Yes, a gorra. His gorra, her slender nose, all her features pulled towards it, her voice fast like lightning. When they first married, she'd take him around to her American friends. Him: so exotic and fun. They had two sons: brown, but fair. For a while it was good. Or maybe never fully good, but bearable. But when the quiet arrived it stayed. Rooted into his bones. The coldness between them, rattling his chest on every inhale. He still gets to see his sons on weekends, lives in an apartment on his own. Her American friends, their selfishness, filling her head with ideas of a divorce.

I divorce you. I divorce you. I—

All the things he's done to keep her from saying it a third time. Divorce. Ya Allah, what people would think. Divorce. He can't even bring himself to think it a third time in a row. So American it bursts his skin to hives, so American it bows his head when he walks by the Pakistani men at the masjid who mutter about his failed business practices: the roofing scheme he tried to start, the gardening venture, the haraam liquor store. His failure: a reputation that clings to him. That clings to his wife. That clings to his sons. Even when he boasted about the great family he comes from. What they were back in Pakistan. Their name, their honor, what they contributed. People would be polite, they listened and nodded. Then they got tired. They would look away. If only he could make more money. Maybe he could see his sons more. Maybe he could see her more. Maybe she'd walk next to him as he entered the masjid.

When his little sister was alive, when they were kids, she looked at him like he could do no wrong. Her eyes big and full of wonder. *Bhai.* No one else had ever looked at him like that. She grew up and got married, had kids, made her own life. And then she stopped looking at him that way. When she died he buried the pain deep in his stomach. Tried to convince his sons to love him while their mom called him a useless sack of shit behind his back.

It's not until his sister's husband dies that his stomach begins to bubble. He realizes how much he's missed that look from when they were kids, how she was the only one who believed he could do anything. How much he missed someone believing that about him. How, through her eyes, he believed it too.

It's sad business, his nieces orphaned a few states away. Sad business, their girlness. Sad business there was no boy among them. Sad business his wife can barely muster an Inna lillahi for. Sad business she doesn't think about as she combs the hair of her two sons, getting them ready for school. Sad business, their dead dad's money up for grabs, the promise of a government check following the orphans until they turn eighteen: 161 checks that could come through for the youngest, 139 for the middle, 120 for the eldest—420 checks total, if they survive.

I don't want them staying with me, his wife says, lounging on the couch. One of their sons is upstairs coloring, the other son beside her watching TV, absorbed in a show where a badly drawn white boy with a large nose, three strands of hair, and an oversized green sweater vest is supposed to be eleven years old. Her two sons are in private school. Her manicured lawn. The Tupperware meal plans for all of them stacked in her fridge. Everything so orderly. Neat and separate—a blessing. Her failure husband is in his own apartment, away from them except for weekends.

When she met him in college, he was brimming with potential. All her friends said he'd make a lot of money. Be an entrepreneur. She loved the stories he would tell; of places she'd never been. How close his skin felt to everything, like he was part of the world and not outside of it. His deep belly laugh, full of fireflies.

It was a gamble, sure, marrying a brown man. But it made her edgy, something she never had been before. She always felt so outside of everything. Like she couldn't even feel the grass under her feet. And then he came, so eager. Her veins started to open. She could feel more, the sun on her arms. His fingers, blending into the soil. A gamble. Even when she stood in front of the Imam, reciting *there is no God but Allah,* removed like she was observing herself, her eyes wandering to the different faces of the men in the mosque, wondering what her life would have been like if she'd met any one of them first. Here, people adored her. They welcomed her, doted on her even. The more she felt how easy it was to be adored, the more her husband's need disturbed her. The more space she wanted. Separate, clean and distinct, a fence around her. And then his mom died. And his sister. Death, how cold it made him. She never fully understood that coldness, both her parents still alive, but so separate from her. He started to become that too: separate. No longer the man that was part of the world, the man she fell in love with, the man she used to envy. He became fenced, lining the walls of his own apartment with boxes like he was cushioning himself against destruction. So no one could get to him. But she couldn't care less, loving how foreign she felt in this new community, how exotic. Her own parents, flabbergasted by her decision. But she had wanted to leave them as soon as she had left for college. Promised herself she would never go back. And now, here she was, in her own house, with her own kids. Her pristine little life. The one she had to claw out for herself. The three orphans, threatening to dirty it.

It'll be like they never existed, the Uncle says, sweaty, as though it's his body placing the marble tiles on the floor, as though he's lifted a finger.

arzoo

I wanted to be her: her straight hair framing her thin face, her high cheekbones and slender nose, her dark brown skin, her long eyelashes calling towards the sky. I would stay up just so I could see her face right before she fell asleep, the moonlight on her cheeks. And when I was sweet, when I smiled just right, she would let me sleep next to her. *My little radiator*, she called me, and so I was: little, radiator, curled to her like a cat waiting to be touched.

God of the playground. God of the eyelashes. God of the cheekbones. And like any good God deserves, I followed her, teetering, calling her name when she walked. *Noreen, Noreen, Noreen.* And unlike most Gods, she answered. She pulled me towards her, balancing me in the air with her feet pressed into my stomach, our fingertips touching as I floated.

She asked for a bunk bed the day our father disappeared for good, when they made us all wear white and all the Aunties came to our house crying. I loved crying. It's what I did best. *Crybaby, crybaby*, Noreen and Aisha would say, and I would cry more. *I'm not a crybaby*, I yelled, my eyes burning, but I knew I was and I hated myself for it. But now, it was okay to cry. I cried, delighted in the crying, and the adults who saw me cried harder, and so I cried harder still because I knew I was a good crier and no one could out-cry me.

———

Your father is gone.

The house filled with the women from the neighborhood, the women who we call Aunty: the one with her round face and thin nose with the gold loop glinting from it, her dimples pressed gentle into her cheeks. Another Aunty, who always smells like badaam and cinnamon. Then the Aunty with the spider hands, skin thin and crackled. And the last Aunty, with yellow teeth and hairs on her toes, who always has caramels in her bag. My father familyless in America except for us girls. But my father familied by the Aunties who picked up the phones and activated the Aunty Network.

Today they crowd our living room as though it is the basement of the masjid, the Aunties holding the tasbihs in their hands, fingering each bead, rocking back and forth.

Your father is gone. What can we do? The Aunties beat their hands into their chests.

Their wails scatter throughout the entire house, frothing the windows, filling the stove, painting the walls. Their wails everywhere, turning our house into a House of Sadness.

A bunk bed, Noreen demanded, dry-eyed, standing in front of me and Aisha. Arms crossed in front of her chest; bully of the playground. *You can get us a bunk bed.* Behind her, me and Aisha tried our best to look tough. Puffed out our chests. *Yeah, a bunk bed,* Aisha mimicked, as I nodded in agreement.

A bunk bed in exchange for a father.

What idiots. He was our father. We should have asked for more.

When adults speak to me:

I'm so sorry for [   ]. You lost a [   ] but you gained [   ].
One night, while coming home from work, your father was stopped by [   ] who had [   ].
Your father was [   ]. Your father was [   ] [   ].
It was [   ]. It was [   ]. It was [   ].
At least he's in a [   ] now. At least he's no longer [   ]. Finally, he is [   ].

To Allah we belong, and to Allah we return.

What the adults mean:

[your loss].   [father]

[an absence].

[murdered].

[a man]   [a gun].

[at the wrong place] [at the wrong time].

[a mistake].   [tragic].   [an accident].   [murder].

[better place]

[hurting].

[at rest].

[To Allah we belong]   [to Allah we return].

Orphans, the Aunties say, and we become something new.

No longer a daughter, no longer my father's kid, but an orphan. Our mom is dead too, gone before I could speak. No one talks about her. Or how she died. Our dad the only parent we knew. Now, orphaned. Each Aunt touches her hand to my head to get her sawaab.

My head, now a home for palms.

Everyone's unwashed fingers comb through my hair. Some of them grab at my forehead, their nails pressing into my skin, as though they'll get extra by prying it open. The wailing in the room so loud it touches Allah. The wailing signaling Jannah, so that the announcement can be known. There are orphans here! Orphans that need to be cared for! Clothe them, feed them, be kind to them. They point to the Qur'an. Clothe them! I look down at the pink dress I've been wearing for three days, pouffed up like a princess. Feed them! My fingers sticky with popsicle. Be kind to them! The hands pushing into my forehead. The new thing I am, taking hold of all my other names.

Noreen ran the playground. Hand on her hips, leg stuck out, daring anyone to step to her. A ball of force, a little sun, so bright it was hard to stare straight at her. Hair wild, sticking out from lopsided pigtails because our dad was our everything: our hairdresser, our chef, our reason for running home at the end of the day. And it seemed no one had ever taught him how to brush hair. We sat in front of him every morning with our mess of nest—twigs sticking straight out, leaves, thin streaks of daal and attah. He would try to run a comb through it, sometimes the plastic breaking off in a tangle, before he put in every sparkly bobble that he could find. Then we'd go to the park by ourselves while he whisked away to work, shouting *Noreen, you're in charge! Stay inside! Follow Noreen!* from his car. And so we did, me and Aisha, trailing after Noreen as she stomped down the street even though we were supposed to be inside, as she paraded through our neighborhood, as the other kids stared from their windows, jealous at how we roamed around by ourselves, how Noreen took us to the park and we didn't have an adult to tell us what to do. And every day, when he would come home we would pretend that we never left and he would beam, *my little Noreen, my little gift.* My father, his whole chest seemingly made of sparkly bobbles, all catching the sun.

After he dies, the body is shipped from Pennsylvania to Lahore to be laid next to his parents, in the land where generations of his family have lived. In the math of what is considered family, me and my sisters are left out. When they close his casket, a VHS is sent to our house, which plays on the TV screen on repeat. A movie of our dead father's bloated face, closed eyes, being put into soil we can't touch. A place he is from, and so we are from, but we know nothing about. On the VHS, in the movie that now plays at all hours, his family members gather all around him. We crowd around the TV and press our dirty hands to the screen.

When the Aunties let us take a break from the TV, the three of us go outside, still dressed in our white kurtas.

I grab a fistful of dirt and throw it at Aisha.
You're dead now.

The soil loud, a stain against what should be clean.

She gathers soil in her fist and throws it at me.
So are you.

And like this, we make our own funerals, burying each other alive, until an Aunty spots us and yells.

The Aunty pulls me to the side, hands me a plastic plate with a bright-orange jaleebi on it. *Your father is gone.* I look at the plate, its soft crunchy edges. *Do you understand? He's dead. He's not coming back.*

Across the room, there is a me who sits by the window, waiting for our father's car. She has my face, the long nose and big eyes, her hair, just like mine, pulled back into a braid. No one seems to notice her, this other me, sitting quietly by the window, eyes on the street. Instead, the Aunty just watches me. Her scratchy hand on my back, her veins blue and spidering down her fingers, trying to comfort me.

But no one notices her, the girl who looks like me, across the room. She taps the window, the oil from her skin blemishes the glass.

Baba's coming back, my other me says, now pressing her forehead against the glass. *Someone took him from us,* she says, and a small flame lights inside me, anger I can't explain. The Aunty doesn't hear, just takes the plate off my lap.

If you go outside, don't throw dirt at your sisters again, the Aunty says. I nod. On my way out of the living room, my other me looks at me again.

You're not gonna wait for him? she asks.

My dad falls asleep at the kitchen table in the middle of the night, tired from work. His long arms over the wood, his head slumped lightly against the hard surface like a pillow. He came back for us. Asleep like this, he looks so young: not a man who belongs to three children and a dead wife, just a man living, just a man who belongs to himself.

Baba. Baba,

we call. Aisha presses her hand into his palm, I snuggle up to his feet on the floor, and Noreen sits across from him. We can't stand the thought of him belonging to anyone but us, even if it is only to himself. His eyes flutter open, the creases of his lips turn up.

Baba! Read us a story!

His spine lengthens, his arms prop up, sweeping Aisha into his lap. Bright. Full of life. The smile spills across his face, so fast you wouldn't know he was just asleep.

Acha, acha. Kaunsi kahani?

When they all think we've gone to bed, the Aunties huddle around the room and grieve loudly. All their concerns pile up between them on the coffee table.

All alone now, the girls—
Who will take them?
Such a terrible thing, to happen to sisters.
If there was a boy, if one of them had been a son, maybe—
No one wants girls—
There are families with sons in Pakistan, they would take them
until they are ready to marry—
What about their Uncle—
He already has two sons.
Yes, but we could try him—

Upstairs, in the bedroom we will leave soon, in the house we will never step foot in again, we all sit on the floor looking at each other. We're a problem everyone's talking about. We make a council meeting and Noreen is in charge. Whenever we're in council meetings it's usually because we need to decide something—to figure out how to ask to go to the toy store, to determine if we're going to be friends with the kids across the street, to see if we're going to walk all the way to the Walnut Street park. Us three, a band of adventurers—making our own rules, deciding what it's gonna be.

———

Girls. They think we're girls,

Aisha hisses, and the word turns to insult. Weak. Useless. Unwanted. I want to be as far away from the word as possible. Sisters. I look up at mine and the word hovers above us, a water balloon threatening to break. Aisha, her name all curves, barely a consonant. Noreen, a hard end. And my name, Kausar, so tough it starts with a pinch. I look at our bruised legs, our scraped arms, our nails bitten down to their beds, the itchy dresses we're forced to wear. Sisters. Alone. Girls.

We're not sisters, Noreen, our leader, dismisses.

We could be brothers, Aisha suggests, and the idea sits between the three of us.

Brothers: a warm word, welcoming even, closer to what we are than how they talk about us downstairs.

Brothers. Outside the stars brother the moon. The moon, our chaand, hangs just out of the window, so close it looks like I could just stretch to touch it. All the trees dangle their branches towards the moon. Aisha sees me staring and gets up, walks over to the ledge, breaking our floor council. She picks up a small figurine I put on the windowsill days ago, a Polly Pocket my dad bought me because I wouldn't stop crying at the store. He loved getting us things we cherished: candy bars, McDonald's toys, a leaf he found on a walk. The Polly Pocket: pink and girly, too much of a sister to be what we are.

———

Someone killed him, Aisha says, her fingers tightening around the Polly Pocket. Like she wants to hurt it. Like she wants to kill it. But it's plastic, her fingers too weak. Aisha looks up and throws the figure up towards the moon.

Hey!

I yell, scrambling up to the windowsill. Aisha laughs, both my brother and my sister, eyes daring me to do something. I look out into the dark for it but can't see anything. Maybe the moon has it now.

You gonna cry about it?

She smirks, dangerous. My eyes wallow, big pools, a tear already threatening to fall as I shake my head. The *no* that escapes my mouth barely audible, barely rising past my chest.

Do something,

Aisha demands. She stands up, hovering over me, a small flicker of rage in her eyes. I cower, trying to make myself tall, but I don't fool anyone—I'm not a threat in any world.

Leave her alone,

Noreen says softly, but a command nonetheless. We look over and see her lying on the floor, her face turned away, her breath pressing against her chest as it rises and falls, a soft whine shadowing every inhale.

A week into the wailing, Uncle ███, our mother's only brother, comes into the house.

Bhai, thank you for coming, an Aunty says, relieved, getting up to greet him.

He's short, with a rounded face and his light brown hair thinned out, almost balding. A big beard with strands of gray hair curling out, and a heavy walk that makes you pause. Fair-skinned, shades and shades lighter than my father, soft sun spots on his cheeks and over the bridge of his nose. He comes holding a stuffed flamingo, pink with long legs. I'm standing by the couch when he enters, the first one of us that his eyes find.

Do you want it?—his voice a delicate singsong. I nod, and he hands it to me.

I'm your Uncle ███. Do you remember me? I look over and spy Noreen staring at him, arms crossed and livid that she wasn't asked first, since she's the eldest and therefore in charge of all of us. Instead of catching her eye I play with the flamingo's long floppy legs. Aisha walks up to him and he gifts her a lollypop out of thin air.

———

You look just like your mother, he says to her—Aisha's face round, dimples in her cheeks. But her eyes are hard, no wonder behind them. She knows she deserves the lollypop. He's a charmer, a twinkle smirks his eye. His laugh booms, the first laugh we've heard since our house became the House of Sadness. It lifts me to my tiptoes.

Stop doin that,

Noreen says, suddenly behind me, her voice sharp like a knife. I bring my heels back down to the ground, eyes to the floor. His eyes focus on Noreen and she stares back, defiant.

I have so much space at my house. I live in a zoo, actually. I got all the animals just for you. I need some help taking care of them. Wouldn't you like that?

Someone who wants us. Someone who came here just for us.

A zoo, Noreen, I whisper, pinching Noreen's hand. We don't have time for a council meeting. It's now or never.

Please, I croon, tugging her arm.

Please please please, he wants us! I plead again.

Noreen looks at me, eyebrow raised. Unsure.

We need a council meeting, Noreen whispers back. My eyes well up again, threatening.

———

No, Noreen. Please, I beg.

Across the room from us, Aisha raises her eyebrow, left out of the whispering.

Let me decide this one time, no council meeting. I close my eyes and think of all the cows, sheep, and lions, of all the space to run.

Okay. We would, Noreen answers, her small voice echoes.

A voice that wavers under *okay* comes back like it's trying to convince itself with the *we would*. Would we? Yes. We would. I looked down at my new stuffed animal. A zoo. Maybe they have flamingos at zoos. I look up to see Aisha, lollypop hanging out of her mouth, betrayed.

Who made the decision? Aisha asks that night as we shove clothes into the suitcases he brought, the occasional Aunty drifting in and out of the room to oversee our packing. I crumple my clothes into a ball and throw it into the suitcase, proud of myself for folding. We don't need this room anymore. We're leaving the House of Sadness. We're gonna have a whole zoo.

Her question oozes with hate. Oozes with hurt. I walk to the dresser in our room and look at the plastic figurines sitting on top of wood. A tiger with faded black stripes, a giraffe, and an elephant with tall tusks that lean upwards. A whole zoo waiting for us, and Aisha is asking about council decisions.

I don't like him, she pushes.

He gave you a lollypop. What's not to like? Noreen snorts, rolling her eyes.

I tuck the flamingo into the suitcase before taking it out and deciding that I'm going to hold it on the car ride. Noreen smiles at me. And neither of us answers Aisha's question, the secret between us.

We stay at the House of Sadness for [   ] days. We eat [   ] and [   ] and [   ]. It's been [   ] days since I've seen my dad. [   ] weeks. I wake up in different places. I get in the car when I'm told. Uncle ████ takes us to see some of his family members in different states, a cousin [   ], another Aunt [   ] and her daughter [   ]. In the other room I hear them say they found the [ ] who killed our [   ]. They put him in a [   ]. His name is [   ]. He needed money for [   ]. How tragic. We go to another house, an Uncle [   ] and an Aunt [   ]. Everyone smiles at us. Everyone is just so, so sad.

Why are you always confused? Noreen asks one day, looking at me. All the adults say I'm in my own world. They'll look for me for hours and find me tucked beside a cabinet, staring at a wall, so quiet they didn't even notice me. When they ask where I've been I don't have an answer. I didn't even realize time had passed. I fall asleep somewhere and wake up somewhere new.

When Uncle ████ finally takes us to what will be our new home, the car ride is hot, sleep drowsing my eyes, making it hard to keep them open. I want to see the zoo and I'm afraid if I fall asleep I'll miss it. Our suitcases are in the trunk, the three of us tucked in the backseat: Aisha stormy as usual, Noreen's eyes bored, fixed on the window, watching the trees blur into more trees.

The Qur'an says if you take care of an orphan, it means you're guaranteed entry into Jannah.

My Uncle breaks the silence, his eyes shift between us in the rearview, the smile light on his lips. His gaze moves to each one of us, his three tickets to heaven, sitting quiet in the back.

Welcome to the zoo, he sings, waking me up from sleep, Aisha's head nestled in the crook of my neck, Noreen's legs taking up half the backseat. It's dark outside, the streetlights spill across the buildings. I push Aisha off me and look around, bleary-eyed, blinking back crust. We're parked outside of an apartment building on a street that looks like it belongs to a city, its wood splintered, interrupting the soft kheer color slathered over the planks. A row of doors stare at us, the chips in their paint like wrinkles, like the old Uncles' faces outside the masjid.

This doesn't look like a zoo, Aisha says, scowling up at the building.

It's not always as it seems, he responds, brushing off his sweater.

The three of us stand together on the street and watch him fumble with keys. Noreen's body rigid, alert, on guard. I hold her hand, my palms sweaty, my head still confused from the dream I was having. I tuck the pink flamingo under my arm and reach for Aisha's hand but she slaps it away, annoyed. She glares at Noreen. The flamingo's head hangs limp under my arm, careening towards the sidewalk. I look at the ground.

Uncle ███████ opens one of the doors and I hear a bird chirp from inside. Zoo? Aisha finally grabs my hand. Her nails burrow into my palm.

A bird flies forward, saffron bellied and blue winged. Cages line the hallway of the apartment building's first floor, but the birds are free, bars spaced too far apart to actually hold them. They fly from banister to banister, shitting on the walls and steps. A dove, a regal pigeon, nearly collides into Aisha as we carry our suitcases in. The birds stretch their wings, taking up space, the apartment hallway fills with their high-pitched songs. Hamsters in cages turn in their wheels; turtles scavenging in their dirty water, bunnies in cardboard boxes sniff out through holes. Everything a little bit caged, a little bit free. *Look, it's a pig,* he says, pointing to a furry black animal that looks like an overgrown hamster. I look down, my foot in a pile of bird shit. Us three at the bottom of the steps, a little bit caged, a little bit free, looking up at the zoo he promised.

In the car I dreamed all the wailing Aunties merged together: a face with all of their eyes, with all of their dimples, with all of their wrinkles. All their faces blend together, until they become a soup of Aunties, until I can't tell them apart from each other. That's all it took: one car ride and they're already slipping from me. I open and close my little palms, sweaty, trying to hold on to what I can remember. I open and close my eyes but it's just us three, in a small room in the apartment that he's put us in. Uncle ███ stands outside the doorway.

Stay here. Tomorrow you can play with the animals. A whole zoo!

He leans forward so that he's eye level with Noreen, his cracked lips in need of Vaseline. His balding head, his sun-spotted face. Fingers through his beard. His one yellow front tooth displaying the gap where his other front tooth is supposed to be. The phone in the kitchen rings and he gets up to answer.

Yes. Yes. Why is he throwing a tantrum? I have the girls, why can't you—

He turns away, his posture slumped.

Can someone else do it? Because, I'm with the girls, his hand on the back of his neck, reddening.

Okay. Okay. No, I'm coming. I'll be right there.

Where are you going? Noreen asks, confused.

I have to go to my family. There'll be someone here for you to-morrow. You're a big girl, Noreen. Nine years old. You can watch everyone, right?

The stress flushing across his face. Desperate. Aisha and I look at Noreen. Noreen, who takes us to the park by herself when our dad is at work. Noreen, who we can trust. Noreen, who is the leader of the council meetings. She nods.

And just as quick as he came into the house, he's gone. Below us, separated by a door, the apartment building hallway is alive with singing birds, the hamsters turning their wheels, the tur-tles crawling towards the water in their cage. Not the zoo that I dreamed, but a zoo that lines the narrow hallway of the apartment building. Aisha's eyes land on me, searing. Like she knows that I am the one who led us here.

Our zoo:

```
┌─────────────────────────┬──────────────────────────┐
│                         │                          │
│      bedroom 3          │                          │
│        (?)              │       bedroom 1          │
│                         │         (us)             │
├─────────────────────────┤                          │
│                         │                          │
│                         ├──────────────────────────┤
│     kitchen and         │                          │
│     living room         │                          │
│                         │       bedroom 2          │
│                         │         (?)              │
│         ┌───────────────┤                          │
│         │   bathroom    │                          │
└─────────┴───────────────┴──────────────────────────┘
```

Fire escape

Staircase and apartment building hallway zoo

In this new room everything can be make-believe. The al-maari looks like my father. Its handle, his nose. The scratch in the wood the dimple that lined his face. The ceiling lamp, our mother. The light switch, her earring. When the light is off, she shimmers, laughing at a party, her earring glints when the moon hits it. I can eat peaches in December, not from a can. I can play outside in our front yard. In the apartment hallway, the birds are rukhs, claws big enough to carry an elephant. They carry us past moats. The bunnies are horses. The guinea pigs are real pigs. We live in a zoo. We once-upon-a-time ourselves.

We once-upon-a-time ourselves. Once upon a time, there were three sisters. Or brothers, maybe. Okay, okay: sister-brothers. Sister-mothers. Once upon a time, they lived in a castle, up high. Once upon a time their father was gone. But once upon a time they knew their father would come back for them. Because once upon a time he was a king. And sometimes, once upon a time, kings needed to do king things, like fight dragons. And wars. And stuff. But kings always came back. So the sister-brothers knew to wait. The sister-mothers knew someone would hear them. Once upon a time. And they'd be found.

The next morning, Uncle ███ sits us down at a plastic table just outside the kitchen, a yellow paisley fabric covering it, soft like a baby chick. We huddle around the table. A closed door next to the kitchen. A closed door behind Noreen. A closed door behind Aisha. A closed door behind my body. Every door closed to us.

Let's go over the rules, he says.

What rules? Noreen asks, cautious.

The rules:

Do what I say
Stay in the room
Don't talk unless you are spoken to
You can only do after-school programs if they are free
Clean up after the hallway zoo
Don't let the birds out of the house
Don't wear anything that shows your arms or your legs
Don't go to the masjid
Pray at home
Don't go to my sons' house
Don't fight your sisters

Don't talk to boys
Get good grades
Go to school
Come right home
Noreen is responsible when I'm not here

When I'm not around and you need to sign something, he says, and shows us his signature on a piece of paper, telling us to copy it.

Noreen and Aisha nod, their fingers wrap around their pencils as they practice. I sit with my pencil and draw a ship that only looks like a ship to me. But Noreen can do it. Noreen can do anything. She wobbles out the *S* of his name, good for a nine-year-old but lacking confidence. He sighs and tapes his signature to the wall so we can all see. *Keep practicing. You'll get it right eventually,* Uncle ███ says. Uncle ███ who drives a powder-blue Cadillac. Uncle ███ who doesn't have a wallet but a wad of cash wrapped up in a rubber band. Uncle ███: the smooth criminal.

Stay inside, he reminds us.

Why? Noreen asks, arms crossed.

His eyes narrow on her, knotting into a fist above his eyebrow that never leaves. His sister's kid. But not a trace of our mother's wonder in Noreen's face, in her skeptical eyes.

———

Remember, it's because of me you're together. You could've been in foster care. His voice songbirded, sugaring the bite.

I tuck my legs under my body and try to sit up straighter. We know what we are. He told us on the drive. Wards of the state. Government property. Orphans. We dangle between this apartment where we get to have each other and a question mark. I look at my hands. I know I can be good. I know I can be perfect. If I follow the rules, then we'll always get to have each other.

That one is your room, he says, pointing to the door on the left where we slept last night. *There's the bathroom,* he says, pointing to the closed door behind me. *Don't go anywhere else.*

When he leaves, Noreen shuffles over to the radio on the kitchen counter and fights with it. She fiddles with the dial until she finds a voice. Michael Jackson. We had a radio in our old kitchen and our dad used to sing along with him. He bought Noreen a green dress once, and she danced to Michael, pleats fanning out around her. Michael sings from the radio, a tiny man inside a big speaker. My sisters are at the table, their chins on their wrists, listening to Michael, too afraid to be the first to move. It's a game, how long we can stay silent and still. How good we can be.

I think of Noreen back in our old house. Before it became the House of Sadness. Our dad swaying his hips, his kurta flaring. The green fabric twirling around Noreen's ankles as she tried to dance like we'd seen Michael do on the TV, so smooth. I break from the table, wiggling my little body. *Annie, are you okay, are you okay, are you okay, Annie?* Noreen and Aisha cackle, and light after me. Our own little rocket ships, launching. We wiggle our legs down the hallway, towards our new room, our terrible voices trying to sync with his.

In the room that Uncle ███ said is ours, every inch of the wall is lined with a bed. Three, for us. One mattress is on a frame, a drawer underneath for clothes. Two others are pressed into each other, unsupported, on the floor. There's a worn blue carpet in the center of the room and frayed green curtains lining the windows. The roaches are so bold they come out in daylight, won't move even when you run towards them. We hear scurrying in the walls, rats, the faint smell of a dying thing just out of our sight. He's put our toys in another room, where he says we can go in and play if we are good. And in the third room, a mattress lies untouched on the floor, set up for someone else.

In Philly we had two floors. The carpeted staircase that brought us upstairs to our room. Our dad. Neighbors with frizzy-haired kids our age who lived above us, neighbors who played with us outside in the grass of the front lawn, neighbors we didn't get to say goodbye to. Here, a five-hour car ride from Philly, it's us and a patch of backyard shared with the other apartments in the building. My Uncle has a bigger apartment where he works down the block, all to himself. He showed us today, in case we need him. But we don't have a key.

I touch one of the mattresses on the floor, the one I slept on the night before. I look at Noreen and Aisha, but no one confirms if it can be mine forever. Noreen paces the length of our bedroom, stacking her feet, counting steps. *Twelve feet!* she says. Aisha leaps up, ready to try, her feet a different size than Noreen's. *No, it's eighteen!* Noreen huffs, hands on her hips, glaring at Aisha. *Okay, it's twelve,* Aisha says, plopping down onto one of the beds.

We hear the front door of the apartment open and shut, voices quiet as a tiptoe. The floorboards creak. Movement. Through the wall, in the room next to us, we hear the voices settle. The three of us look at each other, wondering who else is here.

A gust. Night air rushes into my lungs, rattling my ribs. My throat catches fire. The scream crawls out of my mouth, a large black scorpion. Someone took my father away from me. He was supposed to be alive. My insides feel so hot. I don't know where I am. My arms fire. They rotate, hitting what they can. My tailbone, a stinger. I lash and lash.

I could burn right through my sisters. I'm scorching the floor. Begging Allah to look at me.

I wish you were gone instead of him. I wish it were you, my voice cracks, harsh and dry.

Aisha and Noreen stand in the corner, watching. Aisha's eyes start to water. She bites her lip.

Let her burn it off, Noreen says, arm out, protecting Aisha when she reaches out to touch me.

Don't touch her. She'll hurt you.

When I'm settled, I see Aisha above me. Her eyes, big and slowly blinking, full of questions. Everyone says Aisha looks like my mother. The rounded face, the perpetual scowl, the smokiness around her eyes, her skin lighter than mine and Noreen's.

None of us remember her, this phantom mother. She's a myth. A make-believe. I don't know what she looks like. There was a picture of her at our old house, face round like the moon, small dimples in her cheeks and a duputta wrapped loosely around her hair. But I just see a stranger. My father is turning make-believe too. I'm forgetting things about him: what side of his face his dimple was on, how his laugh curved around the house, the last thing he said to me. I close my eyes, try and remember his voice. The only thing that comes through is static.

We know about the horror movies that start with kids wanting to bring a dead thing back to life. And yet we still clasp our hands together, light the candles we found in the kitchen, and try to conduct a seance that alives our dead parents. The moon hangs low outside the window, supervising us.

Ami! Baba! We yell with our little chests; with all the air we can gather. *Come back to us! Come back! This time we promise we will be good!*

And we mean it, with every fiber that is in our bodies. I know I can be good. I won't ask for more toys. I won't be a crybaby anymore. I won't wail at the bus stop because my backpack is too heavy. I'll carry it myself. Aisha starts to shiver, wriggling her body on the floor, knocking over a candle. The flame catches on a forgotten shirt under the bed, it spreads.

Fire! Noreen shouts, pointing.

I look with my big eyes, useless at the small flame, not big enough to cause any real worry, but still there. Noreen and Aisha jump up, stomping the spread of the heat. Aisha opens the window that leads out to the fire escape, the rings of smoke leave us, leading us into the night. The moon has moved slightly, just out of the window frame, embarrassed.

Do you think I can still wear this?

Aisha asks from the fire escape, looking down at the slightly burnt shirt. Now that it's gone, it's suddenly her favorite thing.

Tum kya kar rahi ho?

A voice, sweet and sharp as a rose, cuts through the night air. Urdu. Noreen and I scramble out of the window, joining Aisha, looking for the source.

And there she is: a woman in her late twenties, her skin a deep brown, duputta loosely tied around her hair, sun moles gathered on her cheeks. She stands on the fire escape outside the next room. She looks like an angel, one we summoned with our flames. The crescent moon dangling in the night sky beside her. From behind her, a man sticks his head out of the window, concern on his face. The three of us stare, our eyes wide. Our candles worked. And what's there isn't horror, isn't a half-dead thing.

We heard about your parents. We came here from Islamabad a few weeks ago. My husband went to college with your Uncle, she says softly. We look at her.

We thought you were asleep so we didn't want to come into your room, but he said he was going to come to introduce you to us. Have you seen your Uncle? the man asks, his voice gentle, like he's trying to not scare us.

Aisha shakes her head. No words, but in the shake of her head is the whole story: our unbrushed hair and scraped knees, the flamingo still in my hand, dirtied from being dragged, dangling precariously from my hand to the ground. They look at each other and then look to the three of us, huddled on the fire escape, engulfed by smoke. I dig my fingers into my palm, my eyes fixed on the couple. Please let them be ours.

Aa jao,

the woman says, extending her hands outward. Aisha is the first to go, walking forward on the fire escape towards her. Aisha turns and gestures for us to follow. Noreen and I look at each other before sprinting forward at the same time. My hands wrap around the woman's leg instantly. She laughs, running her hand through a tangle in my dry hair.

Come inside, beta. I'll fix this,

she says softly, tugging the nest in my hair. I look up at her, our prayer answered, a new mom right on the fire escape. A father in the room just behind the windowsill.

We don't know where Uncle ███ is—if he's in his apartment down the street, or with his family in the house in the suburbs that we haven't seen but that he told us about. But right now, he doesn't matter. He's out of the picture, but there are two new people in the frame.

The man from the fire escape smiles, young in the face, bushy eyebrows. He smells like sandalwood and sweat. His eyes moon. Outside, the moon winks. This time we'll be good. Aisha hangs off his bicep like a jungle gym, gap-toothed smile across her face. They're ours. We're theirs. The prayer, complete.

him

our people love the moon / chaand / our flag yells her name
/ she's always there / a face in the heavens / except for
when she's not / when she leaves / we have to sit with
ourselves / in darkness

when i was young / a boy / i worried she'd leave forever /
i clicked my tasbih ninety-nine times / begging / please
bring her back to us

we belong to a people who love the moon / yes, a god too—
Allah / and the trees as well / the fabric tied to their
branches / their roots deep in the ground / their arms
towards the sky / towards her

every lover talks through her / chaand / every lover
promises / their promises / to her / in turn / she milks
them / she milks me / she tides / makes my blood an ocean
/ at night / the ebb / the wax / the wane / the flow / my
heart / beat / the waves / she moons

it didn't seem strange / until i came / to / america /
where they ignored / sky / where they came / trying / to
find a short way / to us / where they tried / to kill / all
the people / who lived / before / and then ignored / the
moon

when we married / the moon was full / my stomach / hurt
/ too much burfee / drying out my mouth / desert wind /
in my throat / the chaachis / wanting me to eat more /
chaachus wanting photos / stealing my shoes / neighborhood
kids throwing rose petals / abbu yelling / the fabric canopy
coming undone / i couldn't / hear / myself / think

the moon was / full / i was / getting / married / how do
you love? / i asked / under her / teach me to love / teach
me to love forever / i asked / she stared / from her house
in the night / she did not answer / just stayed / there / in
her moon world / doing moon things

seven years later / in america / the moon is full again / by
the foodmart / across the gas station / where the security
guard / danny / always smokes his last cigarette / always
asks me for a light

bright / the moon / her milkiness radiating / out /
lapping towards me / like a warm bath / there are no trees
/ no soil for my body / to rest / just sidewalk / my fingers
/ damp / with my own blood / trying to hold / my body /
together

danny's not here today / the foodmart empty / just me /
my body / blood

there are three of them / my little ones / my sticky children
/ at home

the babysitter / annoyed / i'm not back / inshallah / they'll know / love

so much / the love leaks / out of me / dark red / on / pavement / all I can see

> *the moon /*
> *my blood*

she's full / the streetlamps twinkle / burning more closely / but she still / shines / so full / the easiest thing to look at / i gather / my breath / whisper to the cement

take care of them
please.

blood & not

Like any promise from God, our bargain came late. A year and a half after we moved to our new city in New Jersey, a few weeks before my seventh birthday. A layaway bed, paid for in grief. Uncle ██████ drives around the city, watching the big stores load and unload their cargo. The discarded wood planks. His sweaty body, wrapped in a sweater even though the sun is high and intense outside. He drags the wood planks to his car, mumbling *mader chod* under his breath. He brings them home to us, the loud bang of each wooden plank echoes up the stairs. The birds in the hallway add their flapping wings to the commotion.

What the fuck is he doing? Noreen snorts under her breath. We all stand, arms crossed, watching.

In his hand, a drill borrowed from a friend. His sweater dampens with sweat, the drill screams as he marries the wood planks together. After hours of this, he wipes beads of sweat from his bald head and stands back, looking at the haphazard bunk bed he's built, a painting ladder propped next to it.

I'm not getting on that, Aisha says, eyes daggering the wood of the painting ladder when he leaves.

———

And I know it has to be me, my attempt to show them I can be brave, that I can do it.

I'll catch you if you fall, Noreen whispers, her waves loose and flowing just gently past her mid-back, and I nod. She'll catch me.

I sit on the floor between Aunty's legs as she teases out the nest in my hair inch by inch with a comb. Our Friday night ceremony. She gathers a fistful in her fingers, holding it down so as not to disturb the roots. Her churiya chirp against each other. She presses the almond oil into my scalp and adds rose water down my middle part. Our Aunty. Our pretend mom. The hallway birds' song downstairs, hymn for our ritual.

Our little family—Aunty, her husband, who we call Meemoo, and the three of us. Uncle ▬ doesn't live with us even though he is our legal guardian. He comes around sometimes—to yell, to drop off groceries, but he's not really here. Meemoo is ours. Aunty is ours. But they aren't ours on paper. When we ask them if they can be they say they aren't citizens. Besides, Uncle ▬ wouldn't let them be even if they could.

You call this a massage? Aunty teases.

The pads of my big toes are now pressed into her back, my arms winged. I'm on a tightrope down her spine. Her hair spools out below me, loose curls over the mattress, her palms graze the floorboards. She breathes softly as I walk, as I try to be so light she won't notice I'm there.

Walk harder, she says.

I push down, the soft crack of her back ripples. She laughs and it paints the room.

One day after school Uncle █████ corners us on the porch. We got off the bus with a boy who lives a few houses down from us. He said bye to Noreen and Uncle █████ happened to be checking the mail and heard.

Were you talking to a boy? he accuses, grabbing hold of Noreen's arm outside the apartment door as she fumbles for the keys to the zoo. Noreen, eleven now, and suddenly a grown-up, attracting boys' looks.

He's angry and stares at us so hard it feels like a slap. A quiet man, he doesn't talk much. When he does his spit froths at the mouth. So angry it makes your knees halve in fear.

No, she says, and tries to rip her arm from his grip.

You all are prostitutes. His voice is calm as he looks over us. We three glance at each other, trying to see what he sees, self-conscious in long-sleeved dresses and low-rise jeans underneath. Behind us, the trees turn away, their leaves hiding from his judgment.

We're outside at recess where there aren't a lot of trees. Just sidewalk and a dirt field. All the girls stand by the bleachers and talk shit. The boys roll around in the dirt and call it football. Being neither, being both, I sit by myself in the outfield watching the dust of the baseball diamond rise, its own cloud. Turns out the sky's been the ground this whole time. *Al' Kausar.* There is no gate to heaven, just a waterfall and a boat coasting on a lake. A dock of pearls waiting to receive you. The moon, bright and big. I've never seen a waterfall except in pictures. I've never seen a pearl except in movies. I've seen the moon from the fire escape, nestled in the sky, sometimes dipping in line with the streetlamps. I run my fingers across the fence and make believe it's my dock of grass. Every recess I look for my Kausar, my portal to a maybe-world where I belong. Where there's room for sisters and brothers and some of us in between. Where we can chant and scream and remember every Aunty's name and every mother's face and there are fathers that are not gone.

The bell rings before I can find Al' Kausar and I have to go back into class. In art we're making hand turkeys for some American holiday. I'm the best drawer in class. The only time the other kids like me is when they ask me to draw for them. I do and pretend we are friends. When I hand them their drawings, they go back to ignoring me.

WHEN WE WERE SISTERS 67

Hey Kausar. You like my turkey?

In front of me, Ben's turkey is misshapen. Ben's always the biggest on the field, the first one to tackle another boy to the dirt. When he walks he puffs out his chest and they follow him. He's drawn his fingers too fat. His friends are making fun of him but he laughs. This must be a thing friends do.

It's ugly.

I want to be his friend. But the air is wrong. It's silent, everyone looks at me, faces blank. Surprised. I've never had so many people look at me before. I know I've done something wrong. Ben's eyebrows knot, like right before he's about to tackle. And then his friends explode, laughing.

Oh shit, you're gonna let that freak say that to you?
Who knew she had a mouth?
She called your shit ug-layyy!

I'm in trouble, I know it. I brace my body.

Your mom's ugly.

The boys howl as the words leave Ben's mouth. I watch him lean back against the table, his fists gently pulsing, the vein in his wrist juts out. He smirks as the classroom fills with the ocean of their laughter.

My mom's dead.

———

It's so quiet no one hears me except for Ben. I stare him straight in the eyes. His eyebrows unknot as the boys pound their fists against the desk as their bellies split open with sound, as their whole bodies shake. At the corner of my eyelids, a dock of pearls begins to form. At the corner of my eyelids, a dock of pearls spills over.

Or, the Qur'an says heaven is under a mother's feet. My mother is make-believe. My mother could be the baseball diamond I can see from the classroom window. Another class of kids out there now. The cloud of dust rises as the kids run. My mother could be the grass, what little of it hasn't been trampled. My mother could be a droplet of water from the leaky faucet. My mother could be this hand turkey. My mother could be Ben's fist, gently pulsing. My mother could be the vein in his wrist. My mother could be the pearl on my face.

When I leave to use the bathroom, Ben finds me in the hallway. In school, the hallways aren't rife with birds. I see him coming and try to duck into an empty classroom, but he catches my wrist before I can escape. I see it again: his body against mine, my body cracking into dirt, his fist pulsing and pulsing.

Hit me.

His hand around my wrist is gentle, but firm. I look up at him, confused, but see his eyebrows are unknotted.

I hurt you. Hit me.

Everyone is in their classrooms. The hallway is empty, a ghost town. Ben is in front of me, his hand on my wrist, his eyes pleading. I can feel him on my skin. I've never punched anyone in my life. But I ball up my fist. I drive it into his chest.

Again. I made you cry. So make me cry.

My fist cracks into Ben's chest again. And again. My eyes are on his eyes. His eyes on mine. I'm surprised by how good it feels, my fingers banging into his body, my arm swinging wilder and wilder with each punch.

Again.

He doesn't say it, but I know with each crack of my fist into his chest that he's sorry. With each crack of my fist into his chest, he teaches me how to be a man.

We weren't adopted. And when we asked to be, when we asked to officially belong, Uncle ██████ said no, that we would mess up his taxes, that we brought in money to help take care of us, that we had to stay orphans to keep things that way.

In the mornings we stop by Uncle ██████'s apartment so that he can collect our schedules. Noreen helps me write mine out. Noreen is so smart. She gets A's in all her classes. A collector of good grades. A collector of awards. She's in the special classes for gifted kids. She's so well behaved at school. No one knows our days are organized down to the minute. We don't live with him but my whole day is in his hands.

In the morning, when I submit my schedule, I walk through his living room, stacked with boxes on boxes I can't see over. A small trench he's made, a labyrinth of paper and files that can only fit one person at a time. Different paths to different rooms in the apartment. Each path a vein that pulses. Each path leads back to the center, a heart carved in the empty space between all the boxes. From the heart, I peek out into the other rooms. So many rooms filled with so many papers.

Noreen and Aisha stand off to the side when their schedules are approved. I hand over my paper. A cockroach in the corner of the room ambles lazily across the baseboard. As Uncle ██████'s eyes move over the paper, my breath catches in my throat.

(Please, Allah, don't make me be in trouble.) He slashes the paper. He slashes again.

Across from him dangles a blown-up photo of his sons. They stand in the woods in button-down shirts. A camping trip, maybe; a father and his sons bonding. We've never been camping. If they were around, I'd ask them what it was like. But they're not in the room. His sons don't want us around. He told us that. And so we stay, partitioned from them. And them, partitioned from us. Two sides of a border. Family, but not.

Here, he dismisses, handing me back my paper. We turn to leave. I look back.

There are newspapers laid out in front of him, he's circled the stock numbers, betting. He watches the numbers with the eyes of an ullu, moving money. The TV glow yellowing his eyelids, making him sick.

I need to make more, he says to himself, he says to the TV, he says as he imagines his wife's outstretched arms, his sons in a brand-new car when they're old enough to drive, laughing with their friends: *Oh, this old thing? Baba got it for me.*

I sit on the staircase next to a pile of bird shit holding my paper, crossed out and rewritten with red ink. The poop almost looks like a garbled yolk: the white outside and dollop of black and green in the center. My sisters are upstairs, already doing their chores. A black rabbit with a white star on its forehead presses its nose to the cage, pink nose sniffing, its whiskers dangle out from the bars. A cage down, the hamster runs its wheel, schedule-less. A bluebird lands on the banister and chirps loudly at me. I get up, already tired. I walk to the corner of the hallway and I pick up the broom whose bristles are damp with bird poop.

In the mail, the credit statements start to come, bank accounts opened in our name. *We're rich!* I tell Aisha, pointing at the letters. *We have a bank account!* Our father's money. So many zeros. When we knock on Uncle ████'s door holding the papers, he snatches them, yells at us for checking the mail. *There is no bank account*, he says, shutting the door in our faces. *There is no money*. Aisha checks the mail every day, looking for more letters. They stop coming. The letters must be behind the door of his locked apartment, somewhere in the piles and piles of boxes, the rooms of papers that hold all his secrets. The letters must be on the desk, next to the mattress on the floor. The glow from the TV lands on us, the eyes of an owl.

Ullu ki putti, Aisha whispers and we laugh. Only later I realize we've called our dead mom an idiot.

I didn't mean it I didn't mean it, I swear to the mirror in the bathroom, unsure of who can hear me.

There are checks for us that are coming. He's taking them. I know he is, Aisha confesses to Meemoo as he stirs onions in ghee. The lines in his forehead crease.

It just matters that we're together. You're happy, right? he asks, tugging her braid.

Our dad had money. Where is it? Aisha asks. Meemoo sighs and stirs the onions.

Allah will always give you what you need, he deflects, adding in the chicken.

When we need new clothes Aunty takes me to the fabric store. I touch spools and spools of fabric, the expensive ones with gold stitching, the paisley prints. My Aunt picks a soft yellow fabric with small blue flowers. By the time we get on the bus to come home, the sun is beginning to set. The moon shows up to the party, half full, half gone.

What do you want? she asks softly, her finger twists around my pigtail.

A T-shirt, I say, thinking of the clothes that girls at school wear, the shirts that say GAP loudly, the money to buy them.

Back home, we dodge the birds and their shit in the hallway and I make her tea, balance the cup as best as I can so I don't spill it. Her sewing machine whirs and she hands me the left-over scraps. I snip and cut and glue an outfit for my Barbie: a short skirt and tube top.

She's wearing that? Aunty says, checking my work as she finishes her last stitch on the shirt, examining it to see if there are any loose threads.

Barbie's not Muslim, I say, holding her up to the light, watching her long plastic legs dangle out of her skirt.

In the park, I run after Meemoo, the man who I'm not allowed to call Uncle because the Uncle who brought us to the zoo would be mad. A man I am not allowed to call Father, because my father is gone and I'm still waiting for him to come back. Instead, me and my sisters make up a word to call him, a language of our own. *Meemoo*, we say, running after him as he passes the ball between his feet. Close to the word for *Uncle* in Urdu, but not enough that we would be yelled at for saying it. Nearby, our Aunty sits on a blanket, watching us run, watching us collide. The sun is in love with Meemoo, bouncing its rays off his skin, already brown, but browning more. Meemoo, who used to be a journalist in Lahore. Meemoo, who bursts into a song, lilting *Subhan Allah, Subhan Allah!* when the peach is right, when the juice drips down the length of his finger on the first bite. Meemoo, who now works at the department store a few blocks away, where they pay him in cash and less than the other employees. Meemoo, who saved slowly to buy a car that we can all pile in and drive through the suburbs, watching the leaves change colors. Meemoo, whose parents died before he came to this country. Meemoo, who tells us, *If you don't drink chai with milk and sugar, you don't know how to live life well.* Meemoo, who is an orphan like us. Meemoo, who is ours. Meemoo, who we belong to. Meemoo, ahead of us, running free with the ball, untouchable. Not even when Aisha tries to grab hold of his leg, or when Noreen tries her hardest to run ahead of him, trying to block him. The three of us remain behind until he scores a goal, until the imaginary crowd roars and he drops to his knees in victory and we run, collapsing into each other, into him.

On Valentine's Day we make cards for our parents at school. I ask for three cards. I spread pink and white glitter across them, blowing and blowing, hoping that it stays put. There's a new girl in class, Victoria, who moved from Europe. She has big brown eyes and long black hair swept neatly into a ponytail. She sits next to me and the teacher tells her to make a name tag so everyone can learn her name. Instead of reaching for the markers between us, she takes a clear plastic pouch from her backpack. It's filled with nail polishes. She gently swirls the nail polish brushes, curving out the letters of her name. She paints a mountain in the background, each grass blade its own stroke. My heart hammers. My bubble letter notebook, which made every kid think of me as an artist, is suddenly worthless. Inside my body, a thousand pins descend. Around us, the other kids look over in wonder.

Who taught you how to do that? I whisper.

My mom, she says, looking up, smiling at me. *She's a painter.*

She has a mother. And nail polish. When I move, I feel the pins scraping against the inside of my skin.

I could paint your nails, she says, her eyes focused on her name tag.

———

The pins ease around my heart. I want the gold color, the one she's using to make the sun in the corner of her name tag. But it's too bright for me. I'm not a princess. Maybe something plainer. I point to a clear one. She smiles, putting it in her pocket.

At recess we sit on the blacktop, my hand in her hand, her eyes so close to my nail, examining it from every angle. She brushes the clear paint tenderly. As she paints, she sisters me.

Where are you from? she asks.

Pakistan, I say, though I'm not, but I know it's the answer everyone looks for.

We look alike, a little. Me, darker than her. Our eyes take up the majority of our faces. Her nose is straighter.

I'm from Sofia, she says and it sounds so pretty.

Sofia: a woman covered in snow, wrapped loosely in a shawl.

I wanna go there, I say.

One day I'll take you.

And suddenly: A future together, waiting for us. A future that eases all the pins from my heart, that turns them into ghosts.

After school I tuck the cards between my notebook pages, trying to not ruin them in my backpack. There are no cards for my parents. There are no graves we can visit. No place to put cards. No way they could write back. On my way home I stop in front of Uncle ██████'s apartment. The blue door. The labyrinth of paper inside. I slide out the card and hover my hand in front of his door. My stomach clenches. I put it in front of the door, and scurry down the street, to Aunty and Meemoo, their cards in my hand.

Uncle ▮▮▮▮ takes me with him as he runs errands to the Home Depot and to the bank. He doesn't say anything about the Valentine's Day card, but he smiles at me and I think that means he liked it. I'm a good errand companion: quiet, in my own world, staring out the window. On the way home, he stops at the corner store to buy a lottery ticket.

I stand in the candy aisle, trying to be unassuming but standing close enough to the candy that he'll buy me some chocolate when he finally comes looking for me. The bell of the door chimes and I hear Urdu, two women about my Uncle's age come in, chattering away. They're pristine: crisp shalwar kameezes, duputtas draped stylishly over their shoulders rather than over their heads. When they see him they say their Salaams, before asking about his sons and wife.

Uncle ▮▮▮▮ is careful when he talks, confidently places every detail of his sons' accomplishments forward. It sounds so beautiful, the life he tells, the one where he lives in the suburbs with them instead of in the apartment down the street from us. Antsy, I shuffle out into the aisle, their eyes landing on me.

Oh, is she one of the—

We don't need to say it in front of her, Uncle ▮▮▮▮ says, his eyes sharp, protective, a shield that washes over me.

She's like my daughter, he says, puffing his chest out. And I feel it, like his daughter, how his chest boasts me into love. The only way he knows how. Me, his daughter, in a separate apartment from him, just like his sons, in a separate house. He claims me. I'm his. And I want to be.

Mashallah, brother, you do so much. Their awe soaking the aisle.

The man who killed your father died,

Aunty says to me in Urdu one day when she's oiling my hair,
her fingers gathering my curls and slicking them wet. Died. A
word I've heard all my life, a word I don't understand. She says
it and my body is completely cool, like nothing has changed.
The words feel far away, words I don't understand, words I
can't touch.

He was sick, I think, she adds softly, pausing for a moment. For
the first time I think of the man outside of what the adults say,
what I know he did. Sick. Like when I get sick. Him, coughing.
Plain daal and roti. Someone rubbing his back. My brain feels
far away. A small fog around me. From behind, I can feel her
watching me. Not looking at my hair like she was before she
spoke, but watching me.

Oh, I say, because I know she wants me to say something.
Around us, the air waits. She puts more oil in her hands and
rubs my scalp, before her fingers go limp.

In life, it's good to forgive. And then to forget. Her words are
slow, the Urdu lilting, her hand on my shoulder cautious. I
don't say anything. Let each strand of silence move through
the air, its own curl wanting to be oiled.

The three of us pass the birds that fly above us in the hallway, thickening our ceiling with color. They chirp and we scurry across the steps to avoid their shit. We've prepared our speech, all practiced in the mirror about who should say what. Aunty and Meemoo already asked and he said no. Threatened to report them to the green card office if they kept bothering him. Aunty and Meemoo on a tightrope to citizenship. Me, Aisha, and Noreen are citizens. Therefore, a kind of safe. We make the trek down the street to his apartment cave, the locked door. We knock and there's no answer. Not wanting to go back empty-handed, we decide to do what we know we are not allowed: to go to the suburbs, where his sons and wife live, to ask for what is needed. For what was promised.

Noreen knows the way. He showed her once, in case of emergencies. The bus ride at the end of the PATH and the long walk down the streets with no sidewalks, only grass. When we get there, my legs are tired, Noreen practically drags me behind her.

You're so annoying, she hisses and I know that's my name now.

When we get there and stand in front, I'm amazed. We've crossed the border. The house is a whole house. A neat yard in front, the green moving past to the back where I assume there's more green. The smell of fresh cut grass hangs in the air. A fully leafed tree shades a bench in the yard, surrounded by pink flowers. It's quiet. Not like the shared duplex when we lived in Philly where we could hear the neighborhood kids yelling from the park, and not like the apartment we stay in now with the trees stuck in their designated spots in the sidewalk. This: a whole house, a whole front yard, a whole backyard. Fully grown trees. Their branches dance in the wind. The birds, free, chirp loudly, circling up high. The house belongs in a magazine about houses, its deep brown wood with every shingle in place. A small cluster of flowers by the mailbox, their smell wafts out towards us, watered and alive.

Upstairs, a curtain pulls back sharply and I see them. He is a little older than Noreen, one of my Uncle's sons who we've never met. His hair cut clean and swooped in the front. His face is round just like Uncle ████'s, the same haughty look in his eyes, the glare that flashes when he sees us. The younger one stands next to him. He's about my age, his face thinner, more angular. And as quick as the curtain is opened it's pulled shut again, so fast I wonder if I made them up.

What now? Aisha asks, her toes pointed inward towards each other.

Go ring the bell, I demand, surprised by my sudden assurance, coming out deep within me. And suddenly I feel like I've been stolen from, like I deserve this house, this lawn. Like someone stole my father from me.

The three of us shuffle forward across the lawn, our Payless shoes trample the manicured grass. Aisha sticks her finger forward and pushes the bell, the ring bounces off the walls on the inside and ricochets back to us.

Ring it again, Noreen prods and Aisha does and this time her finger is nervous, the doorbell less sure of itself when it bounces back to us. Seconds stretch out to full minutes, we look at the floor, at the flowers, at the grass, anything else but the shame in each other's eyes.

Her footsteps are so quiet we're surprised when the door opens. The woman, Uncle █████'s wife, is mousy and her face looks like it's pinched, all her features swimming towards her nose. Her pinkish skin draped in a blazer, and salmon nails. Her dirty blond hair is stringy, pulled back into a bun, her mouth a thin line as she looks at us. White, not like us. It's hard to imagine Uncle █████ standing next to her, holding her hand, brushing the hair out of her eyes. Her cubs stand down the hallway in the back. Behind her the counters are spotless, the floors clean. There is so much light in the house, there's nothing to hide.

We need money. For groceries. Noreen stumbles, trying to be defiant, her arms crossed over her chest.

The sun glints down at us, exposing. No moon in sight. I rub my sneaker into the ground, ashamed. Aisha pinches my leg and I wince, standing up straight. And the woman just stares at us, as though she's watching a mildly interesting television program, one that she can't fully remember the plotline of.

When she shuts the door, Noreen sprints away, her long legs carrying her.

Wait, wait! I yell, but all I catch is her hair turning the corner.

When we come back empty-handed, Meemoo smiles. He laughs and picks me up, twirling me in the air. Aunty strokes Aisha's hair, taming a loose curl. *It's okay, beta. We'll find a way.* My hands wrap around his shoulder. His arms suddenly transform into a bed. My legs finally rest.

The next day Meemoo stays out all day, adding shifts to his job. When he comes back home, we crowd around the door, waiting for him. He pats each one of us on the head, tugs at our braids lightly, and falls asleep without dinner.

In the bedroom at night, Noreen and Aisha huddle together on Aisha's bed. They peer up at my flame on the upper bunk. The old anger is there. Layers of new anger blanketing it. I want to hurt someone. My stinger cuts a circle around me. My stinger searches for something to hook into and bleed.

Should we get Aunty and Meemoo? Aisha asks, eyes wide.

Noreen shakes her head no.

I try to focus my eyes on something, anything, that will calm me down. But all I see is Noreen and Aisha, cowering in fear. A stream of thick black smoke fans from my mouth. I don't even know what I'm saying. Still, it spews. This other me, who takes over my body. This me who makes everyone listen.

I'll get you into heaven, I say to the man at the masjid, idling by his parked car, stubbing out his cigarette hastily so his wife won't see before Jummah prayer. It was Aisha's idea to get money from the masjid so Meemoo doesn't have to work more shifts. It's brilliant.

I'm an orphan, I say again, my hand outstretched, the braid of my pigtail coming undone.

Anyone who's willing to love me gets a guaranteed entry to Jannah. I cock my head slightly and tap my foot, seconds slipping until the Azan goes off and everyone disappears from their selective corners, the crack of a hundred knees sounds through the air. The man raises his eyebrow and stares for a moment before a voice reaches out to him, calling his name. His wife, duputta draped around her neck, is on the other side of the parking lot, looking for him like a confused chicken.

I saw you smoking, I say, hand still stretched out, until he digs into his pocket and pulls out a crumpled bill, nearly throwing it at me. Then he's gone, scuttling back towards the woman that he belongs to. Everyone here belongs to someone.

On my way back to Aisha and Noreen I do a double take: there is Uncle ████'s oldest son, his kurta freshly ironed, screaming its newness. A fair-skinned boy, almost white but not quite, wearing Uncle ████'s face. Except for his color, he blends in perfectly with the other kids: parented, monied, belonging. His eyes zone in on me, moving from the bill wadded in my hand to the frayed collar of my shirt. His mother walks ahead towards the masjid, holding her younger son's hand. They don't see me. The older one turns his head quickly and runs to catch up with his mom.

My fingers wrapped in Noreen's hair as she runs and I bounce on her back. Across the street Aisha howls, weaving, backpack dangling lightly off of one shoulder. In this world we were born into nothing but everything is ours: the sidewalk, the yellow markers in the road. The rain falls through the leaves and kisses us just so. What no one will ever understand is that the world belongs to orphans, everything becomes our mother. We're mothered by everything because we know how to look for the mothering, because we know a mother might leave us and we'll need another mother to step in and take its place. The tree mothering its shade. The restaurant door, propped slightly open, mothering its smell of cookies to us. The blinking walk sign, holding on long enough to mother us across the street. The sun mothering Noreen, warming her skin; the sidewalk mothering Aisha's knee, kissing it when her body hits the pavement, a love strong enough to leave a mark. The rain, mothering us faster home. The hallway birds, mothering their cages. The hamster, mothering its wheel. All the mothers in the world reach out to the motherless. And beneath me, Noreen was made to mother me, my heartbeat pounding against her back, shouting so loud that it fills my entire being, *you're held, you're held, you're held.*

Why did you do it? Meemoo asks when we show him the bills we collected, barely enough for a corner store meal. We stand proud after a long day of work. His shame radiates, makes the moon disappear, the night sky goes blank except for the streetlights. And suddenly, our good idea isn't so good anymore.

Of course, his son told on us. Uncle ███ stomps into our apartment, his heavy boots announce themselves on each step, pounding viciously. He comes when Meemoo is at work and Aunty is at the grocery store.

I told you never to go there, he seethes, a small film of spit dangling from the fang of his tooth.

I don't know which "there" he means: his sons' house or the masjid. Both places that are off-limits to us because of what we are, because of how we dirty everything with our touch. Because he gets to be the man with the family and the powder-blue Cadillac, the man who everyone at the masjid now smiles at because he takes care of orphans and his sons are in private school. But if they actually saw us the questions would stack up. Questions about free lunch, questions about our thrifted clothes, about our Payless shoes covered in bird shit.

He looks ahead past us to the door that is closed, to Meemoo and Aunty's room, and I can hear my heartbeat drum in my ears.

———

It wasn't their fault. It was us, Noreen says.

Us, always us. Uncle ███ looks at her for a moment before his hand raises, my eyes find the light flickering gently in the ceiling, a little duller than it was yesterday, as Noreen's whimper reaches my ears.

He sits next to Noreen in her bed, in the bottom bunk. *Why are you acting this way? You are usually so good.* His voice is so calm it pricks the hairs on the back of my neck.

Are you having sex? Are you losing your mind? he asks, eyes drilling into her.

In second grade a girl in my class, LeLe, took our Barbies and put them on top of each other. *Sex,* she whispered, bumping the plastic groins together, their legs intertwined.

No, Noreen says.

I don't even know if Noreen knows what sex is.

If you have sex, you're going to hell, he says, looming over her.

Tum mera dhimag kha rahe ho, he says, the spit frothing in his mouth.

And I see it, his brain being eaten, us three, little monsters, little zombies, gnashing.

And yet, it's a good idea after all, the masjid. Uncle █████ takes it, driving there every Jummah prayer, when the parking lot is so full that people have to park in the Taco Bell across the street. *My sister's kids are orphaned, all alone. I'm taking care of them,* he says to the men as they sip chai, their socks gentle on the carpet. And the men sorrow at the bhai in front of them, a saint for taking care of the aloned. And they go back to their wives, *Can you believe that? Both their parents dead and so young, what a shame,* and the wives open their purses, the shame of death catching everyone in the throat by surprise, as the money flows straight into Uncle █████'s outstretched hands.

Allah is yours, Aunty says, as she teaches us how to pray. We sit on the janamaz with our knees folded. *Allah is yours, you don't need a masjid.* She teaches us how to read the Qur'an on our own after school, the other brown kids in our building come over and sit on the floor with us, each one of us holding a Qur'an. We sputter through the letters. *No one can take Allah away from you,* she says. We drag ourselves out of bed each morning even though I cry because my bed is warm and I miss my blankets. After school the Qur'an is there again and we read, Aunty asks us to recite the same line over and over, none of us getting it right. Soon, the brown kids from down the street come over too, because their parents are working and they need something for their kids to do. Our apartment is filled with little brown kids and their Qur'ans. Amir, who sits quietly in his soft green kurta, looks out the window. Mina, whose nose is always crusted in boogers. Sara with her long hair, frizzing out of its braid. Najma, her voice so raspy when she reads the Qur'an it sounds like a thousand trees creaking. The fan turns slowly, doing nothing to cool us. Our makeshift masjid, our duputtad heads bowed, our voices competing with each other.

My baba says your Uncle ▮ *is a liar,* Amir whispers to me one day in Qur'an class while Aunty sits at the front, having us repeat a single line, all the kids' voices blanketing Amir's.

He says Aunty and Meemoo are your real family. And your Uncle ▮ *is a liar. That he's lying to the masjid and saying he takes care of you.* His big brown eyes search mine, seeing if I'll tell him the truth.

Everyone gives him money for you guys. But they'd stop. If they knew, he says softly, his mouth turned down, sweet.

Maybe I could trust him.

Ahead of me, Aisha's head bobs in her duputta. I think of how a truth could take us apart from each other. How tight my throat has to be for us to stay together. How once a bird learns to fly from its cage, it stays in the hallway. And you can't ever put it back.

Innal lazeena ya'kuloona amwaalal yataamaa zulman innamaa ya'kuloona fee butoonihim naaranw-wa sayaslawna sa'eeraa, I struggle to say, turning my eyes to the Qur'an, joining the voices of everyone around me.

There are slabs of meat hanging from the ceiling at the Halal Market. The smell of old blood is overwhelming, so I stand by the coolers in the back, looking at the mango popsicles. At the front, Aunty counts out the bills in her wallet, her neck craning over the counter, checking the prices. The butcher's eyes flit from me in the back to her.

Baji, you're the one who teaches the children Qur'an, right? he asks, stacking tubs of achaar.

Our makeshift masjid. *Haa,* Aunty nods, still looking at the meat. I move to her, mango popsicle in my hand, wondering if she'll let me get it, or if she won't because then we'll also have to get one for Noreen and Aisha.

Thank you, sister, he says, wrapping the meat, putting it neatly in a plastic bag. He spots the popsicle in my hand and smiles.

We leave, the bag of goat in Aunty's hand. The bills still in her wallet even though she argued with him, tried to pay. Me, concentrating on the popsicle, trying to eat it before we get home, before Noreen and Aisha can see.

Aisha thinks she's ten times bigger than everyone but her fingers are slender and tender. Long too, fingers that she balls up and slams into the pillow. She bares her teeth at the adults and still manages to be cute, still manages to draw their coos out. All bite. All bark. To avoid having to go home right after school she signs up for every free class she can. And that's how she winds up sitting behind the cello, at least twice as big as her. Me, Noreen, Meemoo, and Aunty sit in the audience at her recital, watching all the kids' bows moving in different directions. Chaos. And yet, her bow flows so peacefully along the strings, like water. Her knees cradle the cello in place. She holds it softer than I've seen her touch anything before. The light from the stage hits her just right, her neck long, her eyes fluttering closed, and the song pours from her hands.

It dissolves me, her song. In my mind, a harbor. A boat tied to the dock. The turtles roam. Their little legs crawling them forward through the algae. I could live there, on that boat, the sky clear and open. I don't even need to be bothered. A little bit of food. Some games. A book. The moon. The fish doing fish things. The ocean oceaning. Where everything is so clear.

It's LeLe's sleepover and I fall asleep the fastest. They dip my hand in water so that I'll pee the bed and they can tell everyone that I still pee the bed. Earlier they kept asking where I was from. Where I was *really* from. I cried and LeLe rolled her eyes at me. Now, my hand is in water and their giggles ripple through the bedroom; they wait like lionesses in tall grass. This could be the end of me. I'm fast asleep in my own dreambliss. My fingers expand in the glass, the prints turn to prune. Any minute now the bed will be completely soaked in my own liquid.

Stop, she says from the back of the room, near the closet. Ariel, in my grade but a different class, rubber-duckie pajamas, who would've been the first to fall asleep if not for me. She crawls forward, the other girls watch her with their eyebrows raised. She takes my hand out of the glass, my eyelids flicker open at her touch, her face fills my gaze. She crawls into the bed next to me and wraps her arm around my body, snuggling easily into place. Another sister.

Were you born in Lahore, like my baba?

I ask Uncle ███████, in the front seat of his blue Cadillac, the giant car pulling away from LeLe's house after the sleepover. His hair thin, stranding lightly over his scalp. His bushy beard, graying. Eyes on the road.

No. I was born in Kashmir. Before Pakistan was a country. I came there later.

The light turns red. The car, breathing at the light.

Why did you go to Pakistan?

His fingers grip the wheel. The light turns green. He moves his hand to the radio dial. Fiddles with the speaker.

I don't want you spending too much time with Aunty and Meemoo anymore. People are getting confused about who is taking care of you, he says, eyes ahead.

Just go straight into your room, okay? You and your sisters, he adds, and I stare outside, the trees cut into their small homes in the sidewalk, the cement pressed right up against them, no space to grow.

I fall in love with a boy who wants nothing to do with me. Bobby Perez, with the clouds shaved perfectly into his head. His whole head is the sky and I write his name into my notebook. At recess, by the baseball field, I watch the other boys flock to him. *Bobby + Kausar*, I write with my pink gel pen, looping it in a heart. For our third-grade recital we learn *Ain't No Mountain High Enough*, complete with hand motions. I think of him, his perfect head of clouds above the mountains, canopying the valley. His perfect head guiding the wide river, all my hand gestures in devotion to Bobby.

What are you looking at, Pocahontas?

he says and I lower my eyes and shut my notebook. It's my favorite movie, but out of his mouth it sounds like an insult. She's Indian, I guess, and so am I, I guess. I throw my long braid behind my shoulder and dig my Payless shoes into the dirt, the ones with the four stripes instead of three. I got them praying no one would notice, that my feet would move so fast that the stripes would blur together. But everyone noticed. Aunty and Meemoo didn't understand why I wanted to take them back.

I can't believe she thinks he likes her, Samantha, the most popular girl in class, says, holding court with her friends. They all look at me.

Bobby and his friends run out to the baseball diamond. The clouds in his head are alive, fresh, all that anyone can talk about. I go home and think about it all day, drawing clouds next to each other, stacking them until my notebook is all clouds, until I'm in the sky.

Why do you stay? I ask Meemoo when we make the rounds at Costco, sampling all the trial foods that don't have pork in them. Aunty hovers around the cart, a sparrow around its nest. I think about what their life would be like without us, without Uncle ████'s long shadow looming over everything we touch. A life of always-ice-cream, a life where they get to drive a more expensive car, a life of new clothes. Meemoo looks down at me, his tallness making him a world away, the anger flashing so swiftly in his eyes it surprises me.

Don't ask me that,

he says, throwing the napkin in the trash can. The napkin stained with a hummus from the dip we tried, too peanutty for either of us to like. We walk back in silence, the anger that pulses off of Meemoo taming, a break in the dam. He rests his hand on my shoulder and pulls me in close to him.

You are the best part of my day,

he says, not looking at me, instead looking at the gloves to his right, the ones that are so thick you couldn't even bend your fingers in them. I look ahead and see Aunty in the line, waving at us, asking what took us so long.

On my tenth birthday, Uncle ▮▮▮▮ takes me and my friends to United Skates of America. Noreen and Aisha share the front seat, and me, Victoria, Ariel, LeLe, and three other girls in my class sit in the back. Me, Victoria, and Ariel sit on the floor of the Cadillac, the four other girls sharing the deep bench of the backseat. Every time we hit a pothole the car bumps and all the girls squeal, and Noreen and Aisha cackle in the front. Uncle ▮▮▮▮ smiles, guiding the car smoothly, occasionally checking the rearview mirror to look at us.

At the rink, we skate around and he sits at the big birthday table, following us with his camcorder. Every time we pass him we smile and wave. He's bought us a big pot of tokens so we can play on the machines after, so we can try and get the metal claws to wrap around the stuffed animals they have.

Your Uncle is so cool, Ariel says, holding my hand as we both stumble and try to catch up to Victoria.

I look over at him and see what she sees: the sun spots on his face, his overgrown coat, the tokens on the table, the flash of the camcorder lens as we pass him. His time with us right now, open, unrestricted, a whole universe. Not the kids he wants, but the ones that are around. No wife to dictate the terms. Just him and us. His smile, so bright it feels real.

Aisha practices the cello after dinner, and we all sit and watch her. The bow hitting the string. The low hum reaches the base of my feet and moves up each vertebra in my body. I am on the boat again. The sky is so clear. And above, I swear, I can feel him. My dad. The whole sky smiles his smile.

NoreenAishaKausar! Aunty yells down the aisle of the Block-buster, calling all of us or just one of us.

Stringing our names together, dissolving our skin into one, our hearts line up. We become one heart, six arms, six legs, three heads.

NoreenAishaKausar, she says again and we move towards where she stands at the counter, her finger lightly tapping a VHS tape, as our arms reach out and try to add our VHS "picks" to the collection, as we collide with the aisle display of snacks, nearly knocking it over.

Stop! You make my BP high! Aunty scolds, clutching her heart.

And because no one wants to be the cause of high blood pressure, we abandon our choices, peering over to see what she picked. Horror again.

After dinner, Aunty is in her room in the dark, the glow of the TV on her face. The three of us crawl over to her. She pretends to scream to make us think we got her. I make the popcorn, counting the seconds between each pop to see when it's done, so I don't burn it. All of our hands collide in the bag. I wait for everyone to finish so I can lick the butter off the paper.

It's always a different movie: the twins staring in their matching blue dresses, the photo blotches on the pictures that show there's a demon there, the clown that reaches his fingers out from the gutter. And us three, our names blending into each other, our triple heartbeat, our monstered body, our six eyes looking to our Aunty to see if she's scared.

Too afraid to sleep in our room after the movie, we fall asleep on the floor of Meemoo and Aunty's room, all of our blankets and pillows drawn around us. Aunty and Meemoo, now home from work, in their bed, the square fan in the room trying to cool all of us down. Meemoo's gentle snores pierce the air. Aisha's heavy breath follows suit next to me. Our little family, our little tree homed on the sidewalk, the cement pressing all around us, and yet, still growing.

In the kitchen, the light turns on, Uncle ██████ standing there in the middle of the night. The sudden light waking us all, spilling through the open door of Meemoo and Aunty's room. The dim light catching the top of his head, the brown strands of hair he's combed and set smooth. He breathes and the walls breathe, everything closes in. He takes a step forward. And then another. Each one slow and deliberate, the sound echoing.

Next to me, Aisha is awake but pretending to be asleep. Her arm goes around me. Noreen's fingers twisted in mine. Our three heartbeats lined up perfectly, hammering together.

Meemoo sits up, knowing something is wrong. When he looks around, he sees Uncle ██████ there, a black hole that sucks in the energy around him.

Bhai, what are you doing? Why are you here? Meemoo asks, his voice hoarse, like a tractor has just been run over it, getting up from the bed.

Why are they in your room? Uncle ██████ demands, his voice a bark, an accusation.

Meemoo steps out into the kitchen, closing the door behind him, blocking out the light.

They were scared. They're our kids, bhai, we hear Meemoo's voice, gentle from the other side of the door.

They're not your kids, Uncle ████ says, his voice the hiss of a kettle. My eyes burn, his presence cutting into the little family we built.

So whose kids are they? Meemoo challenges, the air growing quiet around his words.

Aa jao, Aunty says, and the three of us crawl over, curling up into her. She puts her hands over my ears, the sound around me muffles. Everything goes quiet.

Do you know what sex is? Uncle ▮▮▮▮ asks the next day. He has me cornered alone, while the birds fluff their winged feathers above us and croon towards the light in the hallway, a false sun.

I asked you a question, he says, kneeling so that he's eye level with me, so that there's nowhere to look but at him. The smell of his apartment drifts out to me from his clothes, nauseating. I nod slowly, wondering where my sisters are.

Come here.

Down the street we go. To his blue door. Into the labyrinth. I follow him through the paper trench, past the heart, the boxes crowd around me, alive and calling for their mothers.

Sit.

He commands, eyeing the mattress. I'm in trouble. The hairs stand up on my back and I move to sit.

Why were you in his room? he asks and it takes me a second to remember what he's talking about. I don't answer, just look at the floor.

———

It's wrong for you now, to be around men alone. You girls are getting old. Something could happen. And then people would talk, he says, his voice soft, fluffed with concern.

He's like my dad, I say, confused.

No, he says, softly. As though he wonders if I'm paagal. *Your dad is dead.*

My eyes prick, I keep them on the floor. Inside my body hollows.

I thought I told you to not spend time with them, Uncle ██████ reminds me, his fingers tapping on the desk. The papers around all listen. I've broken a rule.

They're my family, the words small in my throat, wavering.

I'll tell the police that man had sex with you, he says slowly.

My body leaves my body and runs through the labyrinth, runs down the street, away from him. The lie he's willing to tell, dangling between us. *That man,* he says, about Meemoo. Like Meemoo is a stranger. That man—my Meemoo, who is working another shift at the corner store and is going to bring me back Airheads when he gets home because he knows I like them. Meemoo, who I would call Uncle if I was allowed. Meemoo, who I would call Father if allowed. Meemoo, who has an interview to get his green card soon. Meemoo, who tells me stories before bed. Meemoo, who tucks me in and turns off the light. My body hovers with the birds, lets them fly onto my shoulder, watching my other body below in front of Uncle ████, still, vacant.

Who are they going to believe? Me or you?

He's looking at me like I'm paagal again. Eyes full of concern. How paagal I would seem to everyone.

I break, fragment, and leave part of myself there.

The next day, Meemoo and Aunty have packed all their belongings into three suitcases. We stand in the hallway and for once the birds don't caw. They hide their faces in their wings, uncomfortable, trying to look at anything else. Noreen cries, Aisha is confused, her eyes moving from Noreen back to Meemoo.

Uncle ███ *says we have to go. It'll be better for everyone,* he explains, each syllable plunging the house into darkness.

All the lights stop working, the gas shuts off so there's no flame. It's daylight outside, but I can't see anything.

You're going to keep practicing the cello, right? You're going to be a star, Meemoo says to Aisha.

Her eyes look up at him, starless. Meemoo's hands find my head, he presses gently.

We'll always be family, okay? Even if we're not together. His voice a soft hug. The creases on his face. His eyes full of water. The tears slipping down Aunty's face. The soft wobble of her lips. *My children,* she whispers, looking at the floor, her hands shaking.

––––––

I feel as though I am your mom, she says, leaning her head against Meemoo's arm, lifting her eyes to us.

Our mom. We'll always be family. Pinky promise. Say it three times in the bathroom mirror. Cross my heart. Hope to live. Long enough to see you again.

Why did they leave? Aisha asks from her bed, her voice confused like when the TV antennas aren't tuned right, when she has to fiddle with the wires to make it work. The cello bow is in her hand and she arches the wood, almost breaking it.

Stop doing that, Noreen warns and Aisha stops. But the bow is still in her hand, like she might start again.

The apartment has been dark the whole day, a reverse night, the glow in the dark stars above me the only thing that I can see. The moon is nowhere to be found.

We're orphaned again.

Uncle ███████'s threat hangs in the air of my throat. I could tell them what he said. But I know they would be mad. They would know that it was my fault, that I didn't stand up for Meemoo. That I let them get taken because of the lie Uncle ███████ was willing to tell. Because everyone would believe him. So, I push it down, burrow it inside of me. It makes a small pit in my stomach, barbed wire around it. The pit is where I put everything I can't say out loud, like how I made the decision to come here, how it was my choice, like how this whole thing is my fault.

What I am: a sack of body that I lug around. Air, water, a little bit of moon. A list of chores waiting to be completed. A bank account in my name. A check from the government. Free lunch. A clothing stipend every three months. Watered and (sometimes) fed so the money will keep coming in. The top bunk of the bunk bed. A house of wails. A house of the forgotten. Aunty-full. Aunty-less. A body and a shadow. A tiptoe across the floorboards. A fingerprint on glass. A small heartbeat, suspended in air. I can take up such little space, I promise. I can be loved. It won't cost you much. You won't even know I'm there.

Who are they going to believe?

[me] or [you]?

[you].

reasons why people go—

Their train comes. They're sleepy. The bell rings. There's not enough food at home. They go to work. They needed money. They wanted to get a toy. They had to use the bathroom. There's someone else they love more. They get pneumonia. They promised someone they would meet them. They hate you. You hate them. They're tired. They ran out of salt. They died. They fell in love with the moon. The birds shit too much. The phone rang. We put them in the ground. You forgot about them. They forgot about you. The bus is outside. Someone else is waiting for them. They disappeared. They work for the government. They don't work for the government. They got fired. They got hired. The British left. The military came. The country collapsed. The country stopped being a country. The land stopped being land. There was food somewhere else. The house got too loud. No one cleaned. We ran out of toilet paper. They got sick. The grass was greener. The grass died. All the plants are dead. No one came. Someone came when they weren't supposed to. They wanted to. They left. They're not coming back.

him

we are in an american movie theater / seated / cold air
blowing / noreen next to me / aisha on my lap / the little
one / at home / sleeping / the screen is full / of what
americans think we are

> *a beggar*
> *loose pants*
> *a topi*
> *no shirt*
>
> *a princess*
> *a pet tiger*

prince ali / *noreen whispers / wipes her nose*

another voice / a small one / aisha
> prince ali / ali a li / ali a la la

her mouth moving / her own language / why did we raise
our kids so far away from what is ours?

will she love him when she finds out who he really is? / *aisha*
asks / fingers clasped around my pinky / eyes cloudless /

love is fickle, *i say / before i can stop myself*
what's fickle? / *she asks / eyes turned towards me*
mader chod /   fickle means it lasts forever

i lie / fireworks / behind aisha's eyes / fickle / like fikar /
worry / both inconsistent / fikar maat */ i say / & she*
stops / worrying

later in the lobby / i struggle with noreen's zipper / aisha
has somehow lost her mitten / we should get something for
your sister */ i say / aisha's eyebrows meet / furrowed /*
she wasn't here

her little voice / daggers

that's exactly why we should get her something

aisha sticks her mittenless hand in her mouth / she looks off /
towards the carpet / she kicks it / seeing if it will fly / it
doesn't

when we get back / the babysitter can't soothe the little one /
she just turned three / & is anxious all the time

we went to go see aladdin */ aisha boasts / the little one cries*
harder / her worst fear / confirmed

not only did we leave her / but we left to go do something
exciting

fikar maat */ i say / but her worry is everywhere / it takes*
hours to calm her down / till all the water has left her body /
through her eyes / her little face streaked with tears /
water-ed out

i put her in her crib / she turns her back away from me /
letting me know she's still mad / even if she can't cry anymore

i tuck in aisha and noreen / turn the light off / close the door
/ i hear / pitter-patter / little feet / aisha's voice / soft

kausar, i love you fickle / i love you fickle / i love you fikar

strangers

As long as there have been Gods, there has been neglect. All our flawed Gods run around, birth the earth, and then forget us. Skip off with each other, talking about God things, annoyed with the banality of our humanness. *I gave you life,* they say when we complain, as they crush the tobacco into the betel leaf, adding syrup on top. *And I can take it away.* Their yellow teeth, gnashing and gnashing. And us, ungrateful humans, fold our knees a few times a day and expect the world to be handed to us. *I made the earth turn. Again,* they say, tired, home from work with a bag of groceries. *But you didn't play with us,* we say and they roll their eyes. Get in their blue Cadillacs and drive away. Go back down the street to their own apartments, where they don't have to think about us. Grow more trees from seeds. Let them branch out to the sky. How righteous, our small rages. *See me! See me!* we yell. *God has to work today,* they say from behind their computers, the dull glow on their faces, annoyed. *We want softness,* we say and turn away from the field of sunflowers that lush their yellow. *Power,* we say and a volcano explodes. *Strength,* and the trees root in their trunks. *Touch,* and the sand clings to our feet. *Allah has forgotten me,* I whisper in my bunk, alone, and I don't notice the moon shining her light on my pillow, reaching.

Aisha returns the cello to school. She stops going to practice.

Meemoo told you to keep playing, I say to her.

He's not here anymore, she responds, the storm above her eyebrows returning.

There's no more music in our house. When I close my eyes, it's just darkness. The night, the harbor, the boat, no longer clear. The sky is no longer my father's face. He's gone. And I can't get back to him.

When Meemoo and Aunty leave, their room is freed up. I'm in seventh grade now, Aisha's in eighth, and Noreen is in high school. We're basically adults. Uncle ██████ brings in someone we don't know, Aalia, whose curly hair cascades to her mid-back. When she talks it sounds like a match lighting, smoke fills up the room. She's in school, she takes the PATH to her college. But I don't ever see her with books, or studying, or even hear her talking about classes. I only see her when I'm in the kitchen and the door of her bedroom is cracked just slightly. Her mattress on the floor, the long cord of the phone dangling over her barefoot big toe, her back to me as she looks out the window, the smoke from her cigarette drifting outside. She's always on the phone, talking to a man she says she's in love with, a man who lives at least an ocean away, a man who also has time to always be on the phone with her. She presses the receiver so close to her face when she's talking to him, her acrylic nails caress the cord as though it's his body.

Uncle ██████ loves Aalia. When he first brought her to the room he wore his best sweater, his fake tooth in place so you couldn't see his gums through his gap. He even put on cologne, his smile nearly splitting his face as she bounded around the house, inspecting the cabinets and the bathroom, deciding if she was going to move in. *Uncle ██████, the hallway is so gross, why don't we get rid of the birds?* she says, calling him Uncle, her voice heavy with honey. He glares at us and I know I'm going to get in trouble for not cleaning it properly. *She's going to college, maybe she'll teach you something,* he says when she is out of earshot, his disdain for us soaking each syllable. He's in our apartment all the time now, every afternoon when she makes them both chai. The huge smile on his face makes him unrecognizable. She putters around the kitchen, the chai steaming in the pot, his eyes on her. When he leaves, we have the rest, the three of us in our room share half a glass, licking the cup when it's done, our tongues searching for cinnamon.

In the morning I watch Noreen tie her hair back, curling iron in hand, trying to morph her waves into curls, coating her strands in LA Looks Curl Gel to get them to stay. The gel is bright yellow, not quite liquid, not quite solid, filled with a million bubbles. She plays Evanescence on repeat as she gets ready, the same song, filling our room.

Bring me to liiiiiiffe, Aisha and I sing and Noreen glares at us.

This is her song and hers alone, she's only sharing it with us because there are no doors to keep us out.

At the bus stop we wait together for separate buses—Noreen's real city bus and me and Aisha's yellow school bus. Noreen's bus, the one that takes her to high school, comes first. Uncle ███'s voice replays in all our heads. *You all are prostitutes.* Noreen lowers her eyes. She gets on the bus. Behind her, the white girls all wear their hair the same, in tight ponytails, not a strand out of place. *Freak,* one of them hisses. Noreen— quiet, straight A student, builder of theater sets. Like Uncle ███, she makes things out of wood. But on the bus, no one cares what she can make. Noreen's eyes are on the floor. When the bus pulls away, she doesn't look at us.

With Aunty gone we've stopped reading the Qur'an. The other Muslim kids stop coming over for prayer. Uncle ███ brings us to a new teacher, his friend who was an Imam. Our new teacher is too old and blind to see Aisha nodding off behind her duputta. He insists the sound of the scripture can never be ugly, even as it struggles and sputters in my mouth.

What the fuck, Noreen mouths across from me, as I sound each Arabic letter out loud, fumbling through the shortest surah in the book.

In my mouth, the Qur'an sounds like I am dragging roadkill. Aisha's head lolls on her neck, a big-ass lollypop careening on a plastic stick. This is when my sisters hate me most: when I'm wasting their time, prolonging the hours they have to spend covered and in this hot room, under the foul breath of an Imam so old we think he might die at any moment. *Fa-fa-saal-lie-lee-li*, I try, my voice a high whine, a cat in heat.

Aisha's lollypop head finally gives way, and she slams forward into her open Qur'an. She startles herself into a fart, like a backed-up car engine on the street. Noreen's cackle sparks the dead air and suddenly all of us are on the floor, laughing, tangled in our duputtas, our Qur'ans forgotten on the tables. Our fists bang the floor as we try and steel ourselves, our Imam still at the table, shaking his head.

Make it last, make it last, make it last, my heart whispers to itself. The three of us sit in a circle, quiet, looking at each other. The first to laugh is the first to lose. My sisters, my Gods, my mirrors. *Make it last, make it last, make it last.* This feeling. Aisha and Noreen looking at me. Their eyes soft. My heartbeat syncing with theirs.

Aisha and Noreen don't even look like sisters: Aisha's skin fair, a light brown, dried out under her heavy-lidded eyes, Noreen's skin a deep brown, always dewey, glowing. But looking at them now, they blend together. They blink the same, heavy, deliberate close. My sisters watch the world closely, only shutting their eyes when they need to. My sisters bite their lips the same, hold back the laughs in their throats the same. My sisters can make anything last: the salt on the crackers enough to hold our bellies over for dinner, the shower water we use one after the other, the blanket stretched when the night gets too cold, the silence in the room, the eye contact: brown moving to brown, daring one of us to break.

We cut through the park that no one goes through, the one where Aisha says rapists hide in bushes waiting for girls to walk alone at night. The sun peeks beneath the trees, looking over us occasionally. I'm not exactly sure what a rapist is, but I know it has to be bad. Noreen says it's someone who does something to your body that can't be undone. But it's not night, and we're not girls, we're brothers or sisters or mothers, or somewhere in between, so we walk deliberately, spread out, our little fists ready in our pockets, daring someone to try us.

When we get to the dollar store, we survey the goods. Everyone knows not to pick up anything on the first lap of the store, how dangerous it is to get attached to the first thing you see. I walk each aisle carefully and contemplate everything as though I could really buy it—the microwaves, the DVDs, the toilet brushes. But I know what I want. I find myself in front of them, skin glowing creamy, whittled-down waists, bow-legged, plastic ankles. I pick out the least expensive, holding her like a prize.

We meet back in the corner by the plastic plates. Noreen has a lipstick and Aisha a bag of Tootsie Pops. *That's $3.99,* Noreen says, looking at my Barbie. I don't point out that Aisha's bag is $2.50. The audacity of a dollar store to sell things that aren't a dollar. Aisha rolls her eyes. *She doesn't even have tits.*

We walk out in silence, me carrying a lipstick that matches Noreen's. *You're too old for dolls anyway*, Noreen says in the park as Aisha darts ahead, already sugar-high, three Tootsie Pops in. When we get home, I try on my lipstick, rubbing the bright red-orange across my chapped lips. It makes my mustache stand out, my goatee curls under the pigment.

See? Noreen says, without even looking at me. *So pretty.*

In the mirror, a soft layer of fur lines my top lip. A small patch of hair lives underneath my bottom lip, the size of my thumb-print, a dark furry half-moon that greets me when I see myself. What I remember of my father, I can see in myself. The dimple in his cheek. His big-throated laugh. Every morning when I wash my face my hairs look up at me. The hairs whisper *man, you're a man* and I nod back because it's true, because I hear them call my proper name.

One day Noreen comes home with a garbage bag she swings proudly.

Coven meeting, bitches!

I get off my bunk, ambling down the rickety ladder, Aisha rolls off the mat, flopping sideways on the floor.

What's in the bag? Aisha says, eyeing Noreen suspiciously.

Shut the fuck up, Aisha, and I'll tell you.

Noreen huffs, pissed that Aisha is stealing her thunder, pissed that Aisha is not instantly grateful at the arrival of a random garbage bag full of unknown things that now live with us. When I finally make it down the ladder and clamber into my place in the circle, Noreen dumps the contents of the bag on the floor, splaying them out.

Fabric. Mesh. Sequins. A pile of dresses. I pick up a short black dress, Aisha examines a tiger-print halter top.

Dress up, bitches!

Noreen coos gleefully, throwing us the dollar-a-pound clothes, clothes Uncle ▇▇▇▇ would never let us leave the house in.

The things I do for you. The things I do!

Noreen yells, wonder through each syllable, before she collapses onto her bottom bunk, staring straight ahead.

I'm the best fucking mother ever.

The black sequined dress falls right below my underwear line, my twelve-year-old legs already furred with hair spilling out underneath the fabric. It's tight around my middle, only to have a gaping hole where the chest is, made for someone with enough titties to fill a cup, where I only have puffed-up nipples. My feet tap the rhythm of *Playas Gon' Play*, the song Noreen is blasting from her boombox.

You can be your own Barbie.

Noreen smiles wide, her eyes dancing. I look in the mirror, at the gap between the dress and my chest, my hips stretching the fabric. My shoulders too wide to be a doll's, but I become one anyways.

On the other side of the room is Aisha, wearing the tiger-print halter, arms out wide, looping circles, her eyes closed, face pointed up towards the ceiling. And I wonder what she's made herself.

We were made for each other: We were made to duck and weave past the birds as they swooped down low towards us. We were made to show off our supplies to each other: the old T-shirts from the school's lost-and-found stashed in our backpacks, the scissors from art class. We were made to make thin strips out of the T-shirts, to fasten them to the top bunk like theater curtains: us, our own set, characters, and story. Aisha was made to steal the bat costume from the school play, to prance around in it in our room while Noreen hoots from her bunk below, the perfect audience member. I was made to be the rain on Aisha's bat skin, which is to say I was made just so I could pour the glass of water on her at exactly the right time. Her shriek was made so it could hit my ears, so it could cue Noreen laughing so hard she's dry-heaving, gasping for air, her feet kicking anything in reach. Noreen was made to pee the bed just then, the wet of the sheets the only thing stopping a rain-soaked Aisha from braving the painter's ladder, from climbing up to my top bunk. Aisha was made to scream *You peed! You peed!* through the room, her voice a high whistle scratch, all nose, like it was glued to the roof of her mouth. Noreen was made so she could hobble out from the bunk, pee-soaked, collapsing onto the floor, shouting *You stupid bitches* between her dry heaves. And we were made to be each other's perfectly stupid bitches, fastened to each other, forever.

Out of the darkness, in the room that used to be where we played, comes Tiffany. One day she isn't there and the next day she appears, shuffling to the bathroom, head down, not looking at us. Our toys outside the room in a box. *You're too old for toys anyway,* Uncle ██████ says when I ask him about it. Aalia ignores her, staying in her room. Our Uncle says Tiffany's a science professor, or she used to be, before she came to America. Our city is full of Used-to-Bes, of people who came from somewhere else, whose degrees don't matter here, who check out groceries and pump gas and return to their single room in a rented apartment, to a framed photo of them in their cap and gown holding a degree above their bed. Tiffany doesn't talk to us, she just shuffles along quietly, and when we're in the kitchen together she's so still that my breath feels rude.

I watch Aisha move through the house, her basketball shorts down to her mid-calves, her T-shirt a tent she lives in. At night she opens the window and slides onto the fire escape. The moon nowhere to be found. She walks barefoot, the metal cutting into her skin.

What the fuck are you doing? Noreen calls.

It reminds me I'm alive. Aisha's voice, husky, blends into the wind.

Beyond our room is the night. I watch it from the top bunk. If I reached out, I could touch it, I could be a part of it like Aisha. And beyond our door, Aalia and Tiffany—two strangers we share a home with. Our world is ours, and if anyone else knew they'd take us away.

But maybe it'd be better. I dream, briefly, of a father not-gone, of someone who helps me with my homework, not that I need it, but just to be there. Of his voice, un-stranged. His voice telling us stories. How he met our mom. How he fell in love. Maybe we could live in our castle. Maybe we could have an adult that comes home to us, that pulls up in our driveway.

Or maybe it'd be worse.

Noreen. God of the Real. God of the Orphans.

Noreen hates high school. All the people crowded into the hallways, trying to get from one building to another in less than four minutes. Noreen shoves her books into her backpack and walks forward with her eyes to the floor, her only two friends flanking her side. Whenever she takes a step, she hears it: the people whispering *freak*, the walls pressing and pressing until there isn't space to breathe.

There are good kinds of pressing and bad kinds of pressing. A good kind of pressing: when the three of us are sleeping in our one room, the wood of the bunk bed pressing into itself, Noreen in the bottom bunk and Aisha in the bed I can see from my perch, our breathing pressed together.

The hallway is a bad kind of pressing for Noreen. The bus is another bad pressing, everyone's hands trying to hold the same railing, all the bodies pressing into each other, everyone pressing *sorry*s into each other's ears but not able to prevent their bodies from bumping into each other. When she comes home, there's no space to breathe, our bunks too close, Aisha on the mat next to us, all of us breathing the same recycled air, the house of strangers outside our door pressing in, threatening to open.

After school is the only time that she looks up, when her legs bring her around the track at practice. When she runs, her lungs press against her chest and her legs press hard against the pavement. There, with her body struggling to get the air in and out, is when she feels most alive, when suddenly the space around her multiplies itself rather than divides.

If I had a superpower, I'd make more space. I'd make the air multiply. I'd make the hallways multiply. I'd make our bunk bed multiply. I'd make us have so much space that we would only have to touch each other when we wanted.

Above me is space, below me space, between Noreen and me: space. Noreen has so much space around her, even when we share a room, even when my body becomes a cat, a little radiator for her to steal heat from. There's so much space in her eyes, black holes that I can't touch. I wonder where it came from, how it stole into her.

Aisha is making her own space too, even when she sits next to me, I don't know where she is. In some other body, in some other world, in some place I don't have the key to.

In school, they talk about science. About space and planets. But everything is make-believe. Mars could have water. Pluto could be a planet. Could not be. There are things in space that my teachers can't explain: black holes that can crush a sun, suspended air where nothing moves. I wonder what crept inside Noreen, what space crushes her. All around me, my classmates have their own planets, balls of lights that they orbit.

And us, at home, a different breed: born alone, born together. My sister-mothers. Untethered. Me, waiting for them to come home.

All the girls in my class brush their hair into smooth braids. Their fingernails are clipped, painted, and glittering. They carry purses and have an extra pad *just in case*. They all wear lip gloss, have hairless legs, sit on the bleachers, pop gum. Their gold hoop earrings jingle when they walk, their eyes and lips lined perfectly.

To me, Noreen seems like a girl who blends into all the other girls, who can line her lips and blink her eyelashes real slow. I think she's the most beautiful person I have ever seen: Noreen, a girl through and through, a girl without being any part make-believe. Noreen looks over college brochures after dinner. She dreams about leaving here. *When I go to college, things will be different.* At the bus stop she looks at the ground. I don't know why she lowers her shoulders. I wonder what about high school does that to a person. Maybe I don't want to know.

MISSING PERSON

Name: Tiffany Kim
Last seen: Bridgeway Crisis Intervention Services
Date of Birth: 02/13/66
Age: 35
Sex: Female
Race: Asian
Hair: Black
Glasses: Yes
Height: 5′ 5″

Warning: this person can be a danger to themselves and others.

If you have any information about this person, please contact:
[   ]-[   ]-[   ]

One day when we're walking home, the neighbor across the street stops me and Noreen and tells us that they saw Tiffany go into our apartment. They hand us a rain-covered paper, the kind that's plastered to trees and empty walls in the neighborhood.

That night, we put it in the middle of the three of us, cross-legged and barefoot. We twist our necks to get a better look, careful not to pull on the ends of the paper so that we don't destroy it.

It could definitely be her, Aisha's voice, maybe almost positive.

Yeah, I think so too, me, trying to agree with anyone.

I dunno. Could be anyone really, Noreen, the voice of reason, hand on my back.

And then we hear it, loud and low, the start of a whimper from down the hall, the far back of the apartment. A whine, almost feral, avalanching to a full-blown howl.

Tiffany the scientist, Tiffany the Used-to-Be, Tiffany in the back room of the apartment, Tiffany the howler.

And then the three of us look at each other and fall over, unable to help ourselves, the laugh breaking the fear, escaping our bellies, so fast that I can't breathe.

Aalia always wears dresses and jewelry, the smell of jasmine following her when she walks. Her makeup isn't from the dollar store: it comes in shiny packages that get delivered to our apartment, little bits of confetti to cushion its journey. Or else my Uncle brings it to her, little gifts he presents her with as they sip their chai. Noreen scoffs, jealous. I stand in the kitchen, taking extra long to wash the dishes so that I can watch Aalia as she dips her brush into the yellow pressed powder, drawing it across her eyelids.

Come here,

she says and I didn't realize it was so obvious that I was watching her, that she could feel me staring. I slowly put the sponge down, wiping down the sink, nervous. My small feet guiding me into her room, the one that used to be Aunty and Meemoo's, towards her, where I stand behind her and we look at each other through the mirror that she's propped up against the wall. She smiles, warm, honey-sweet.

Tucked neatly on her desk is the missing person's paper that she found in our room, that she showed Uncle ████. *I'm not living in an apartment with an insane person, Uncle,* I heard her say, Uncle ████'s lips turning into a frown. And after that, Tiffany was gone from the apartment too, missing. And we realized then: Aalia has the power to make people leave or stay.

She gently plays with her silver ring, slipping it off her finger
slowly.

Here.

I put it on my finger and look at it contrasted against my brown
skin. It shines, makes me less dull.

Lip gloss is for biotches, Noreen says at the dollar store and I put the small vial back, the girls in my class who wear lip gloss now all in a new category I didn't know existed. Noreen gets me a bright red, something with "fire" in the name, and I think of my lips ablaze, catching. I want to paint our whole room with it and let it all burn. Noreen puts it on first, her lips so bright that everyone looks when we walk through the park, Aisha drags behind us, fingers raking the fence. Noreen laughs with every nerve in her body, a laugh that wakes the park, a laugh that makes the men lean out of their windows and smirk as we walk by. Everyone asks Noreen where she's going, where her body is headed, but she doesn't answer, only takes my hand and twirls me around the park like I'm her little top, spinning, spinning. And I spin and her laugh bubbles again and the fire is all across her teeth, smudged onto her chin. And I don't tell her, even though I know her face will fall when she looks in the mirror and sees. I love the red like that, how where her lips go the color follows, how her fangs are painted with it, threatening to drip fire or blood or love, depending.

Uncle ▉▉▉▉ sits at the dining room table in his best sweater, completely ignored. Aalia is on the phone again, only this time it's during chai hour, and there's no chai in the pot. And when Uncle ▉▉▉▉ gets up to leave, soundlessly, he shoots a look at the three of us so terrifying it slaps my bones. We scamper into our room and spend the rest of the night in silence.

I think of the lumpy family portrait I had painted in my mind: Aalia and her chai next to my Uncle and his smile, and the three of us, pushed to the background, but still there.

A few days ago something happened on the phone that made Aalia cry, that made her plead *but I thought you loved me* over and over. Then she stopped going to class. She stopped taking the PATH anywhere, stopped leaving the house. She sat by the phone and called and called. He wouldn't answer. She stopped dying her hair with mehndi. Her hair full of grease.

He doesn't even want her. Can you imagine being that desperate?

Aisha snorts, trying to shake the fear, and we all roll over at the same time, backs turned away from each other. All of us in our separate beds, in the same room, imagining trying to convince someone you're worth their love, someone who used to make chai for you, someone who spends her life waiting by the phone, someone who's forgotten you exist.

One day when I'm in the kitchen, Aalia's door is open. I peek inside and she's gone—her body and all her stuff. The apartment emptier. Full of memories of the people who used to be here. Uncle ▮▮▮▮ stops coming around.

We watch the planes drive straight into the buildings. The pillars of smoke. From above, it looks like they're smoking out an ant house. On the news, people run through the street. At night, the door of our apartment building is spray-painted. *Terrorists.* A few days later *anthrax* is written across my locker. My shoulders cave forward at school. All the Muslim kids avoid each other. Ariel bargains with her friends at lunch on my behalf: *she's one of the good ones, I promise.*

My stinger burns around me. I want what is mine. The same old flame of anger. Inside, I heat. I feel so dangerous, like I can't keep myself in my body. Everyone looks at me like at any moment they think I could blow. Like I could boil over. Like I could spit oil. Like I could burn anyone close. I need help. I need an adult. And I don't know how to get one.

The TV always tells stories that aren't true: white girls who live in space, the plastic of their dresses never wrinkled, rolling their eyes and sighing *mom* like that word could ever be anything but sweet. There are movies where people who are dead come back to life. Where they really just were missing the whole time. There are books I read where orphans use magic, see their dead parents again. I want to find Al' Kausar. I want to hear my father's voice. The last time I saw him was on the TV, his body being lowered into the ground. I tell Aisha and Noreen and they agree. Aisha nicks a light from a bike she found on the street; we put a water bottle and the light into her mini-backpack for later. I insist that we have to go at midnight. I spend every ounce of my energy keeping my eyelids open as they droop, as my hunger for sleep threatens to ruin my plan.

It's time.

We get up, not bothering to change out of our pajamas. Aisha slides the window open and we all crawl onto the fire escape. We slip down the grate, tumbling out onto the concrete of the street, the only sound Aisha's backpack clanging lightly against her back. The moon is full, flashlighting us. She beacons the sky.

Noreen says there must be a way to the other side. It would seem like we would need to find a tree, some woods, something in nature we could reach through. But we live in a city, and all around us are buildings and paved sidewalks, the dim rumble of a car nearby. Noreen, God of All of Us, takes the bike light and clips it to her shirt. We follow its blinking red when the streetlights go out, when the night is plunged into night.

Noreen's legs are long, and her body can carry her faster than mine. The light is harder to find with her bounding ahead; I trudge into the darkness. I'm not careful; my foot lands in a pile of dog shit, I feel it mush under me. I wipe my shoe frantically against the grass, trying to get it off. But I can smell it as I walk, the stink of waste flooding my nose. A trail of flies follow me, flitting around my feet, marking my body with their hunger. My sisters are far off, in the distance, lights I can't follow. I swear I hear something. A voice I haven't heard in a long time.

Baba? Baba.

I spin, looking. I heard his voice. I know my father is dead. I know I'm too old to believe otherwise. But something takes hold of me. A hope I never knew I was holding. I know I've seen the VHS tape of his body being lowered into the dirt. But maybe it was just a movie. A make-believe. Maybe he's just lost. Maybe he's in Al' Kausar. Maybe he has other hims like I have other me's, maybe he left one behind that's been watching us.

I've seen them do this on the news: When they're looking for someone, they make a team of people to find them. They call their names and shine their flashlights into the trees. But there are so few trees. And I don't know my father's name. I don't know his voice. But I need it now, more than ever. I need him to talk to me. I spin, calling the only name I know, offering it to the city. I spin and spin, the flies spin around me. He was supposed to be here. My father. But that man took him and then died. All this fire inside me I can't get out. All the people who are responsible for it, gone. I raise my arms to the sky, I offer them my body to give me my father, whatever part of him still exists, back.

The sky does not open, the bike light does not hit a figure waiting for us, no woods appear to help our search. It is just us three on the street, our pajamas too thin for the winter, flies whispering in my ears, my sisters staring at me sadly, like I'm broken, like I'll never be fixed, the bike light blinking a dull red.

What the fuck is she doing?
Just let her do it.
Does she actually think our dad is alive?
Aisha—
She's twelve, Noreen.
It's not that big of a deal.
I told you this was a bad idea.
Stop being a dick.

In Aisha's voice, I hear it all: my stupidity, all the time I've wasted believing in a father that does not exist.

———

I turn, and there she is: Aisha, the slight dimple by her lip dancing, the streetlight flickering in her eyes. Suddenly, everything is laughing at me. The sidewalk, the trees in their cement cages, the leaves, the mailboxes along the doors. Everything is laughing. A thousand laughs that wrap around me, that start to suffocate all of them. And there's Aisha, standing in the middle of it all, her laugh the conductor at the symphony of laughs, her laugh making a magnifying glass of my emptiness, her laugh that, when held to the light, bursts my body to flame.

They knew.

They let me guard my little pile of garbage on my own, they let me love a thing that could not be.

Each cell in my body multiplies, a hot wave that starts in from my cheeks and spreads down to my feet. The streetlamps become spotlights, and I, my embarrassment, center stage.

They knew. They knew.

Before I know it, before I can really understand what I'm doing, my shit-laced feet carry me straight to Aisha. I want to hurt her so bad. I want her to feel what I feel, what's always inside me, what I try and tame. My stinger is alive, pointed, ready. My fists ball like Ben's and drive straight to her neck with all the anger my body can muster. I'm alone in this world. And my only family is laughing at my need.

No one loves you.
You're the reason they're gone.
They left because of you.
Because no one can stand to be near you.
Who would ever call you their daughter?

Aisha's face breaks, a dam overflowing, a faucet that needs fixing, not from my fist, not from my nails clawing at her, but because I've said the unsayable, because in the saying, I've made it truth.

Who are they going to believe?

[me] or [you]?

[me].

The next day I realize what I've done when Noreen won't look at me. I grab Aisha's arm.

Hit me.

Aisha tries to shrug me off, but Noreen looks over, confused, interested at the display. Like Ben, I puff out my chest. I hold her wrist gentle, but firm.

I made you cry. So make me cry.

And when she does, it's not scraggly like my punches. It's well aimed, straight to the stomach, so hard that I think I might never breathe again. She descends on me, hands at my face. Hands at my neck. Her nails draw blood. It's the knife in her eyes, like it was always there, like how when it came, I could no longer recognize her face without it.

I show up to school with the scars, fingernail dents in my face like crescent moons. Ben comes over and sits next to me.

Where did you get them?

My sister-mother. My other God.

Please tell me you fucked up her face back.

Aisha's face scarless, beautiful. Her furrowed eyebrows. The pout of her lips turning down. Annoyed, but intact. He shakes his head and gets up, heading towards his friends.

Always go for the face, Kausar. Always the face.

I think about Meemoo and Aunty—I try and remember their faces, so they don't disappear like the Aunties I remember loving but cannot name. Every night I practice what it feels like to be loved: Meemoo swinging me from his arm. Aunty learning to ride her bike next to us. Aunty braiding my hair after oiling it. I keep their love inside me, pack it into a small jar. This is what it feels like to have a family. See? I had one too. And then another. Even if they're gone now. It has to count for something.

The hallway animals have lasted longer than any of them. They outlasted Meemoo and Aunty. Tiffany. Aalia. The animals owned the hallway before any of us came, picking the locks of their cages, stretching their wings past the bars. They chirped along with our cries. Turned their backs when we complained too much. Shat, always. *They should be free*, Aisha says, her finger strumming the bars. Last week, a rat crawled into the hamster's cage and scratched its face bloody. It breathed slowly for a day before dying. Two months before, the guinea pig died without reason, curled in the corner of its cage. The hallway is not safe. They're dying, and we can't protect them.

A green finch cocks its head slightly and looks at Aisha. All our animals, our zoo, our tiny tiny Gods. The only thing separating them from the sky is the door we have the keys to. The three of us look at each other, uncertain, shifting our weight from leg to leg. *If they're really ours, they'll come back*, Noreen offers, advice she read from a book somewhere. It sounds true. We nod, our council decision unanimous, silent. Aisha opens the door. The birds look at each other, at us. I pick up the bunny, put it on the porch. It turns to me, the sun touching the white star on its head. *Go*, I say and no one moves. *Go!* I yell, and the birds take flight.

Uncle ███████ dismantles the bunk bed.

I'm going to move you soon, he says, wrenching wood piece from wood piece.

He slowly takes out the planks, placing them next to the trash cans. From the fire escape, I look down at the hunks of wood.

A bunk bed in exchange for a father.

What idiots.

We should have asked for more.

him

*it's not that i don't love her / it's just i didn't know her and then
she became my wife*

*

*red lengha / henna winding like a tree / around her fingers
/ soft ringlets braided down her back / laced with flowers /
gold glints against her skin · / the modest chain connects her
ear to her nose / her brown skin / dark and smooth /
catching the night / her eyes down at the ground / our eyes
find each other's / through the mirror between us / i look at
her reflection / not at her / study our faces together / what
a lifetime of our faces will be / around me / everyone else
does it too / the math / what our kids will look like / they
come up to us / quiet / & say*

mashallah

*

*in america my apartment is too small / uncomfortable / when
we go to the park / she walks around / befriends all the flowers
/ she walks and walks / checks behind each rock / the base of the
trees / when she's found them / the ones that she's deemed perfect / she whispers*

i'm sorry i'm taking you from your home

and plucks

*

*her hand on my knee brings me back / her body stretched on
the bed / the moonlight on her skin /* what's wrong? / *she
asks / & i count all the things / the apartment too small /
twenty-three years of a life / a wife / & my emptiness / on
my lap /* i have nothing to give you / *my voice / the crack
in its root / a rotted tree*

    daughters
    i want daughters

*her curls spread out on the sheets underneath her / her arm
dangles out over the mattress on the floor / taps the beams of
wood below / a fly buzzes nearby / lands on my shoulder /
her voice / an offering /*

    i'd want to name one noreen

*noreen / said in my wife's mouth / the syllables heat /
blend together / i brush the fly away / it flits into the air /
abuzz with the name /* noreen / *i say it to myself / trying
it out / the fly moves over to the window /* I watch it without
watching / *noreen / a beautiful name*

                noreen
                i try it again

                noreen
                i could live with that

a lord

a fly

My nipples have exploded into puffed shapes that stick out under my shirt. Aisha and Noreen have their periods, a portion of our allowance is allocated to pads. Mine hasn't come yet, but I carry a pad in my backpack because Noreen told me to. *Worst thing would be to walk around with a bloody ass,* she says, nose snarled like she knows I would be the type to walk around with a bloody ass. We're grown now. I'm about to go into my freshman year of high school. Aisha is a sophomore. Noreen is going to college. My father is dead. I won't look for his voice again. I know now.

Uncle ▬▬ says we're expensive. With Aalia and Tiffany gone he decides to move us so he can rent out our apartment. He puts us in a narrow one-bedroom apartment in the basement. There's no door separating the bedroom from the rest of the apartment. The bedroom is smaller than the one we had upstairs: it fits a twin bed and a trundle holding another twin bed. When the bottom bed is pulled out you have to crawl on the beds to get anywhere in the room. There's a small hallway and a kitchen that opens into a living room. He's gotten us a computer, stacked on a tiny table by the couch in the living room. And three Nokia cellphones, where we can call people for free after nine.

See? It's all brand-new, he says, gesturing to the marble countertop.

Aisha hits my arm and I look up to where her eyes are, the electrical circuits come out of the ceiling. On the other side of the unfinished basement, separated by the laundry machines and gravel and rocks, is a two-bedroom apartment Uncle ▬▬ ▬▬ is building. As soon as he got the toilet to work a college kid from Pakistan named Omar moved in. He sleeps on a small cot Uncle ▬▬ put up. He blurs words together when he talks, soft and low, making you lean in to listen. Aisha has a

crush on him. *Hi, Omar,* she says as we pass by him near the
laundry machines, lingering extra long on the *O*. The paper
clip in his ear, a makeshift earring, catches the light. His apartment is not his, just the cot and toilet, and his university books
stacked neatly on the floor. There's thick construction plastic
all around his apartment that looks like Saran Wrap, curtains
of it taped all around. Like everything is in a refrigerator, but
it's not cold, more like sitting on the counter waiting to spoil.

There's only one room, Noreen says, looking at the one bedroom we're now in, crossing her arms.

*You're going to college. It's enough space for you all. And you
have to share the kitchen with Omar,* Uncle ███ says, already
annoyed at our complaining, his eyes moving to the door as he
thinks about what else he needs to do.

When he leaves, it's us three in the apartment. No threat of
him bringing a stranger in. No new Tiffany. No new Aalia. No
zoo to maintain. This place is just ours. Except for Omar, who'll
need to use the kitchen. But at least he won't be sleeping here.
Aisha sinks into the couch, looking out of the window to the
street. I go over to the computer and touch the mouse, the
screen awakens.

Okay, this is kinda cool, Noreen says and we all examine the
new apartment, our freedom.

All my friends live a room away from their parents. In the
same apartment, or in the same house. They report to their

adults. We report to each other. Teenage-adults. Our zoo is gone, and we're on an island alone. Uncle ███████, in a helicopter above, occasionally flies over us. Dropping down food. Sometimes landing to use the computer.

I'm not paying for you to go to school, you have to get scholar-ships, Uncle ▮▮▮ says and she does. Noreen gets into college in New York City on a full ride.

There isn't space here for your stuff, you're going to have to take it with you.

We celebrate by packing her stuff into his car, cramming it so full that there's no space for me and Aisha to ride along. We know when we leave from here, there's no coming back. No space to put our things, no home that will be ours to return to. When I leave, he's going to rent out the apartment. And the three of us will float in space, only tethered together by our silent strings linking us to each other.

Noreen is going to college. Uncle ▮▮▮ calls his rich cousins and their kids who live a few states away that we sometimes see over holidays to brag about her. *Noreen is going to college, mashallah she's so smart. I raised her.* Noreen is leaving. She doesn't have to be a sister-mother. She can just be Noreen. The space between us lengthens and lengthens. I reach for her and only feel wind.

When I arrive to high school, it feels different. I am neither liked nor unliked, I am just there. People smile at me in the hallways sometimes. Ariel, LeLe, and Victoria try to make friends too.

I say hi to people. When people call me their friend, I put their phone numbers in my cellphone. For their birthdays, I decorate the lockers of the people who say hi to me. They decorate mine back. In this school, only Ariel, LeLe, and Victoria know my parents are dead. No one else knows. Or knows where I live. I could be someone else.

I practice being normal. I say my parents live at home. They work late, so me and my sisters are alone a lot. But they love me. I have my own room. And they give me money. And they keep the fridge full of groceries. I become a new me.

My new friends call me shy, but they buzz around me. All of us, little flies that circle each other. When I raise my voice to speak, they are surprised. Most of the time my voice is sucked out of the room, caged in my throat. There's a lot of things that I keep there: the dried-up sounds of the Qur'an, all the good jokes that I think of too late, the letters to Noreen about how much I love her.

At home, my constellation of sister-mothers is broken. Sometimes Noreen comes back from college on weekends but mostly not. Aisha feels far away from me. I can't recognize her anymore. She stays out with her friends from the swim team. When she gets home she's on the computer, doing her homework late into the night, irritated when I try and talk to her. My sister-mothers are both on their own boats, in different seas. I'm waiting at the shore for them to come back. I don't know where my boat is, or where my sea is. My body looks wrong, my hips a little wider, my breasts pushing out of my chest. I look for my own boat, something that can take me away.

Sophomore year Bobby Perez is in my physics class, the boy who used to have clouds in his hair. There are about twenty-five of us in the class, enough for me to disappear. He is still the most beautiful thing I've ever seen: his cheekbones high as mountains, the piercing in his left ear glinting across the room, his warmth sunning everything. He knows exactly what he is: a boy with no other bodies that live inside of him. A boy who moves with the confidence of the sun. A boy who shines.

I'm waiting for my bus at the station when he comes. Bobby Perez. Cool enough to wear a Spider-Man backpack to high school and not get made fun of. With the Adidas wristbands that touch his skin. *Hey Pocahontas,* he says, the first time he's talked to me since we were kids on the blacktop. We live in different directions, but he waits with me anyways and says he'll run for his bus if he sees it. He talks about Ms. Adams, how he thinks he's gonna fail the physics test because he can't remember the equations. I don't know why he's talking to me. Probably because I'm smart and he wants to cheat off me. *That's your bus, right?* he asks as the 84 wheezes up to us like a grandma. I don't know how he knows that. *Yeah.* We watch the passengers line up. Slowly, everyone gets on, pays their fare. *You getting on?* he prompts, and his eyes fix onto mine for the first time. *I guess not,* I say and we both watch the bus sputter away from us.

It's still now, our side of the terminal empty, the air heavy with what I've just done. In the distance, I see the 10. *Yours is here,* I let him know, because he's still looking at me. He barely blinks. *Oh,* he says, not even a breath, so quiet I almost miss it, as his ride home crawls away.

The next day Aisha and I take the bus to the fabric store Aunty used to take us to. When we're in the terminal I think of Bobby, how he looked at me. How close his hands were to mine. How time slowed down. Aisha is annoyed and says I'm not paying attention in the fabric store, complains about how I didn't say anything to her on the bus. We pick out a long black piece of fabric. When we get home, Aisha goes to Omar and tries to flirt, puts her hand on her hip and flutters her eyelashes.

Omar. Is there a hammer in there by any chance?

When he gives it to us, he's polite but wants nothing to do with her. Aisha sulks as we go back to our own apartment. Balancing on the kitchen stools, we pin the fabric to the opening of the bedroom. The fabric becomes a door that guards our bodies while we change, while we sleep.

In the morning, on the other side of the fabric partition there are men. Their voices seep towards me and my eyes open. Uncle ███████ is hosting men in the living room. They talk about construction, their Punjabi thunders through the apartment, electric and alive. *Why are they here?* Aisha mutters, half asleep. Through the haze of the fabric, through the haze of my sleep, I see them move. Their bodies a slow dance, a swaying on the couch, the kiss of a teacup to lip. Even this one-bedroom apartment isn't fully ours, we're afterthoughts in the back room. All around us men pile up. I have to pee. But I don't want to leave our room while they're here. Their shadows big, their voices swallow all the space in the apartment.

At lunch when I walk by his table, I hear Bobby tell his boys *that's my heart right there* and they all look up at me, watch my body pulse lightly, watch my face rose with embarrassment. It's in my cheeks now, the red creeping under my brown skin.

In the bathroom I examine my hands, my long fingers. I look at my eyes, *bug eyes,* Noreen calls them, how they take up half my face. My cheekbones, small peaks. I stare and stare, but can't find another heart to give. Just mine: a little of Noreen's, a little of Aisha's.

When I get to class, he winks at me. He's laughing, his whole being a sun, everyone is tethered to him. I want to go up to him, tell him that he's wrong. His heart isn't with me. Or maybe I misplaced it. But I'm not sure when he gave it to me, and it doesn't seem fair: to be responsible for something that I didn't ask for.

That's my heart right there.

And my stupid brain won't stop replaying it, on repeat, over and over. And maybe it's not such a bad thing, to belong to someone else. To be someone else's body.

Were you and my mom close?

I ask Uncle ███████ one day as he tinkers on the pipes under the sink, trying to fix a leak. I can't see his face, it's under the cabinet. Just his legs, sprawled outward, the hole in his sweater moving with the rhythm of his arms, the thin white shirt underneath.

We used to be. When we were younger.

I try and think of him young. His brown hair full and cut close to his scalp. Peach fuzz on his upper lip. All his teeth in place. His face, unwrinkled.

And then what happened?

A pause as the hole in his sweater stops moving. His arms still. The air on standby. For a moment, I think he might answer.

Stop asking me questions.

Bobby is with his boys again. Everyone is outside before school, milling around before the bell rings. The wall is like the watering holes in the nature documentaries our teacher plays in history class. The cooler you are, the closer you can get to the wall. And there he is: sitting right on it, perched like a lion. The sun hits his face so his brown skin glistens, his friends framing him. He could be a painting in a museum. A last supper.

We're so far apart it doesn't even feel like we're in the same school. I burrow my hands into my jacket to keep them warm; Aisha took my gloves this morning. I stare out past him, towards the library, its small steeple nudging the sky. I breathe out and watch my breath collect outside my mouth. I don't know how he can look at me the way he did two days ago when we both ignored home, and completely ignore me today.

It's as if I don't exist, which is, I suppose, the way it's always been. When the bell rings everyone breaks apart, the packs separate, moving towards class. He's off the wall, arm around Kareena, his boys all circle around him. Kareena is beautiful: long black hair gathered into a long braid, her round, smooth cheeks, mole dancing above her lip, her medium-colored skin. When she moves through the halls everyone parts around her. And worst of all, she's so nice that I can't hate her. She says hi to me every morning by my locker, remembers my name, smiles when we pass each other in the hallway. She seems like a girl who wouldn't talk over me when I'm around her, a girl who would make space for my voice. Of course, his arm would belong to her.

My legs are so slow today. They feel like they've been punched by a thousand Kareenas. I feel it again: The dull flame inside me, the want to be in someone else's skin. My skin cursed, too hot. I lumber up the stairs, past the mounds of discarded chicken bones that seem to always be there no matter what time of day. By the time I make it to physics, I'm so tired all I want to do is go home and sleep again. We're making wind turbines as our final projects, calculating what angle we would have to make our blades to harness the wind. Across the room he laughs, and I force myself to not look. My body feels sick, too hot. My body threatens to dissolve into flame and around me everyone works, completely unaware. I ask to go to the bathroom. For a second, I think he watches me leave. But when I turn to look, he's talking to Adrian; I must have imagined it.

The hallways are empty: smooth, sterile, where minutes before they were so full of students trying to get to class I could barely breathe. Complete chaos and complete stillness. Everything moves like this. Emptied, it looks like a hospital room, which is maybe exactly what I need. I lean my head against a locker, its cool steel calms me. The smoke of my body dissipates, my feet are on the ground. I exist. I touch the locker, my fingers tracing my name into it. I am here.

Are you okay?

———

And there he is, brown eyes a well of concern. I turn, my back against the locker, and he takes a step towards me. His eyelashes are so long they look like mine, like they could reach out and touch me if they wanted. He's too close, I can feel my head swimming again.

I don't feel so good.

I put my hand up to keep him away from me, but he ignores it. He presses against me, my hand flattening between us. I can feel his breath on my neck, his fingers moving around my waist.

My voice is gone, off somewhere I can't reach, flattened against his chest. I try and push away from him, my body so hot it's scaring me again. He grabs both my wrists in one of his hands and holds them. I can't move. I had no idea he was so strong. His other hand slips up my shirt and I whimper, squirming. No one has ever touched me like this, his fingers slide up my stomach, hooking under the padding of my bra. My knee jerks against him, pushing against his thigh, and he presses his body against mine, into the locker.

Stop. Do you wanna get me in trouble?

Deep inside my chest, I feel my body unpin itself from my body. I step outside myself and watch my other body slump against him, her eyes on the floor, watching the tiles. I don't want to go to hell. And I don't want to get him in trouble. So I walk down the hall, marveling at how still everything is, while his fingers slip into the waistband of my other body, while he moves aside her panties, while she gets so quiet it's as if she doesn't exist.

Back in physics I sketch out my blade. Across the room, all his boys take turns smelling his fingers. *That's my heart right there.* Their laughter is so loud they're getting scolded by Ms. Adams. *Honestly,* she huffs. I don't want to look at him. I put my head down on the desk, feel the coldness of it against my neck. When Ms. Adams comes over to ask if I can put my head up in class, I tell her I don't feel so good. I feel his eyes on me. I think about how my blade will be made of bamboo, soft and tender to the touch. How it'll catch the wind, how it'll be able to move off of just one breath.

I'm not hungry today, my stomach pressing in on itself so much it's painful, so I skip free lunch and sit in the grass. I grabbed a juice, something I thought would make me feel better. Everything has been so loud and I just need some quiet. Something feels like it has been taken from me, but I am unsure as to what it is. I think of how he looked at me like I belonged to him. I think of my smell on his fingers. How he showed his friends. I belong to him now. I know if I ask Aisha she will be mad at me. I pick up a twig and prod the dirt. A family of ants work together to build a soil condo. I watch them scramble over each other, carrying specks of food towards their home. Even ants have a home. Even ants have family. I take out my juice and pour it over them slowly, watch them all drown, pinching each one that tries to escape between my fingers.

I wonder how many bodies unpin themselves from their other bodies, how many bodies have multiple bodies inside. Like Aisha, who sometimes gets so sullen she stops talking, in shorts so long they look like sweatpants, shirts so big I wonder if there's a body under them at all. When she gets like this I call out *Aisha, Aisha,* but she stops answering to her own name, just stares through the fabric, waiting.

After a few hours, she'll come back, changed into a thrifted yellow sundress, smudging Noreen's dollar-store makeup against her lips. And this too is an Aisha I have never seen before, an Aisha with collarbones and breasts, an Aisha who teeters in her friend's heels and smokes Black and Milds on the sidewalk, an Aisha who is part of the world instead of above it.

Noreen has another body too. It moves with her new friends at college, laughing, joking. Noreen's other body has left us behind. She can blend in easily, can pretend us away. The shortened story of us, almost an afterthought; *oh yeah, my two sisters.* As though that's all we are, as though we aren't everything in each other's entire worlds. Noreen's other body is smoky around the edges, just like the night. If Noreen's other body had a name it'd be something short and sweet. Like Noor. Almost what she could have been born as, what she's decided to become now. She comes home on weekends and our apartment isn't good enough for her. *I should've just stayed in the dorm*, she says, *the dorm* rolling so casually off her tongue. Aisha and I stare at each other, annoyed at Noreen's escape.

Whenever Noreen's other body comes back, she sleeps in late. She brings us food from her meal plan. Bread, chicken breasts, mac and cheese. I peel the crusts off the bread and roll the middle into a white ball. I eat it that way, the bread so dense it feels like a full meal.

Now that the apartment next door is finished, Omar is gone. Uncle ██████ kicked him out so he could rent it for more money. A new Pakistani couple is in his place. My mind a confusion of people who come in and disappear. I can't keep track.

When it comes, it comes in the toilet. So late I've been pretending to all my friends I've had it for years. The clots are almost dark brown, chunky. Mixed with pee and water they swirl, expanding and collapsing, inhaling and exhaling, jellyfish of blood. I kneel on the floor and watch them, like toilet tumbleweeds. It didn't even hurt. Just moved through me, almost unnoticed.

Noreen is at college. I don't want to call and bother her, so I go bother Aisha instead.

I got my period, I say, my teeth crisping an apple, trying to get Aisha's attention as she sits on the couch.

Do you want a fucking cookie? she asks, not looking up from her book.

Sometimes Uncle ██████ is there and sometimes he's not. When money's good, when he's bought a stock that's paying off, or when he's bored, he comes around. When he does, he helicopters. He hovers—asking us questions, demanding to know our schedules, annoyed that we didn't clean enough. He takes us to Costco, tells us to stock up for weeks, and buys us groceries. He takes us and our friends out to Old Country Buffet and pays for the whole bill. He brings us home knockoff Gucci bags he got from his trip to New York. He grills outside sometimes, charring the beef to the wellest of well-done. *You don't ever want to eat the blood,* he says and we nod, our plastic plates filled with mushrooms and chutney. When he's there he sees what we're cooking, he slides his plate across the counter to me and I heap on the pasta and burnt tomato sauce. When he's there he gives us money for Taco Bell or for the pizza place down the street. He stands outside with his camera and films the squirrels in the back of the apartment building, narrating each of their movements. The way they bound on top of the bird feeders, eating all the seed. *You've been sad without the animals,* he says and gives us ten dollars. The three of us take it, surprised that he noticed. We ride across the city to my friend Dominique's house, take a kitten from the litter her cat just had, a small fluffy black-and-white one. Name it Oreo. We cradle the carrier between us as we take the bus back, the kitten's soft meow whimpering.

When he's there he drives us to soccer practice. He drives us to our friends' houses. When he's there he brings his friends to the living room, knowing that he can't take them down the street to his apartment, so crowded with boxes of paper that there's barely room to walk. They sit on the couches and I say *Salaam, Uncles*, as I pass, moving towards the bedroom where I can be alone. *Salaam, beti*, they say and through the curtain I hear them talk about how smart I am, and mashallah, what a good girl I've turned out to be. He tells them about Aisha, says she'll be ready for marriage soon. Aisha scoffs, tosses her hair over her shoulder. *I'm not getting married to any of their shitty fucking sons.* When they leave, he sits at the computer, the glow on his face as he clicks and clicks. As he follows the stocks. *Okay, we're going to bed now*, Aisha says and he nods as the both of us file into our room, thankful that Aisha had the foresight to get the curtain. Aisha and I share the twin bed. When Noreen is home from college we pull out the trundle and she sleeps there. *Why is he still here? He has his own apartment down the street*, Aisha says and I roll over, annoyed that there's four people in a one-bedroom apartment. Annoyed that what separates us and him is a thin piece of fabric. Annoyed that our Uncle has so much space for himself and yet he still comes for ours.

When he's not there, our friends crowd the apartment. Victoria and LeLe lounge on the couch, Ariel on the floor, Aisha on the stool. The square fan on the floor cools us, each of us fight to sit in front of it, yelling into it as it distorts our voices, bending them around the apartment. We're girls alone, and they all want to come over so we can talk about sex without anyone around. Not that we know anything about sex, just the stuff that we've seen on TV. *You can fuck someone but if you suck a dick then you're gross,* Ariel says and we nod. *If you fuck naked you're gross. You should wear a shirt,* Victoria says and we take note. Nakedness equals gross.

Aisha and I look at each other before looking away. Our shame brings us into ourselves. Fucking. We don't talk about fucking. Fucking is something we learned from the Qur'an not to do, learned that if we do Allah will be mad at us. And Allah is already mad at us, because he took away our parents and Meemoo and Aunty, so we know we don't want to make Allah madder, in case he takes away anything else.

The key to not making Allah mad is not talking about it, is letting everything go unsaid. But here go our friends, talking about fucking like we should all know what fucking is, like fucking is for everyone.

Our groceries run out and Aisha uses the money she's been saving for college. She works at the T.J. Maxx during summers, and slides in shifts around swim practice and meets. We called Uncle ███████ to ask for money. He got annoyed and hung up the phone. Aisha kept calling. He didn't answer. An endless phone tag. He forgets that we need food. He forgets to feed us.

You're so expensive, he says, except we know his sons have been in private school their whole lives. The government gives him money for us each month. We know our dad left us money. He opened up bank accounts in our name. We watch him sit in front of the computer, examining stocks, his skin gaunt from the glow, transferring our dead father's money from account to account.

We could make so much, he whispers to himself, the whites of his eyes tinged yellow. Oreo meows and weaves around our legs. We stand in front of the open fridge, stare at the bare shelves and wonder what we can make of what's in the kitchen cabinets. Ramen seasoning on Doritos. Zebra Cakes. Andy's hot chips. Three-day-old jawbreaker. Push Pop. Bagel. Cream cheese out of the container. Peanut butter. Moldy bread. Cereal. Pasta sauce on saltines. Can of soup. Go-Gurt.

Warheads. SpaghettiOs. Half-eaten can of tuna. He says he'll pay us back but he doesn't. Oreo needs cat food. Her litter box smells and piles up. We forget to clean it. My sisters are the adults of the house, running everything. *Make it last, make it last.* And we do.

Aisha in the driver's seat of Uncle ███████'s powder-blue Cadillac, window open, fingers playing the wind. Me in the passenger's seat, feet on Aisha's aqua battery-powered boombox, blasting Ja Rule. Uncle ███████ is somewhere—in his apartment cave or with his family—and left the keys to his car on our kitchen counter. And so, like a responsible sister-mother, Aisha told me to get the fuck up and get in. Her legs peeking out underneath her basketball shorts, her hair pulled up in a ponytail. Free, my sister. Not thinking about groceries, or college money, or if I ate lunch that day. Just a girl who belongs to the night. Just a girl who's stealing a car, taking it for the joy. *You got a girl that'll ride ride ride,* she sings along to Ashanti, our sideburn queen, our hope. The smile breaks through on her face, like the sunrise opening into pink. My sister-mother, my other God—younger than Noreen, but a God no less. A God in her own right. God of the night; God of the stars. God of the boombox. God of the wind in her hair. Driving, over the bridges, the streets winding out before us. Us two, in the car. The whole city, ours.

I stop going to the bathroom in physics. I stare straight ahead and still feel his eyes bore into me. Most days it's easy, he's with his boys, or his arm is draped around Kareena and I know it's okay because there are other people there to fill the space. She is the girl he puts his hands around, openly. I am the girl he puts his hands inside of, privately. We are different but in either case he is the victor, he always has a girl that his hand can find. My hands are tangled in each other under the desk. Uncle ████ said I had piano fingers, surgeon hands, like my mother.

It's been so long it seems Bobby's forgotten about me. After school he's at sports and I'm at theater, so we're not at the bus stop at the same time. I sit so far away from him in class. We are in different jungles. But then one day, outside, I see him arguing with Kareena. She's crying, but I can't hear what she's saying. He looks sad, reaching out to her, like he's trying to get her to stay still, to look at him. But she won't. And then he stops walking with Kareena. He stops draping his arm around her.

I can feel him watching me. The more time that passes, the heavier he stares. He sits closer and closer in class until he's right behind me. For a week, he doesn't say anything. Until my name is on his mouth, a small song he whispers. *Kausar. Kausar.* Maybe it's the portal I've been looking for. Soon, all his friends are doing it, a little chorus behind me. My name, sugar sweet on all the boys' lips. I know if I don't make him stop, he's going to get me in trouble.

He finds me in the staircase after I leave class. I know it's dirty but I don't trust my knees, so I sit anyway, next to a discarded burger bun someone left behind. He comes in and I marvel at how his body seems so sure of itself, how he takes up space. His hands are in his pockets, his chest open; my hands are tangled into each other, all my bodies caving in on my chest. He never looks down; he never drops his shoulders. I can't tell if I'm in love with him or if I want to be him.

Why'd you stop talking to me?

I'm surprised by the pain in his voice, his arms crossed over his chest like I could hurt him. I'm surprised by the way his eyes go soft, the ripple in his jaw as he bites his tongue. My mouth is so dry I can't imagine saying anything. I think about his arms around Kareena. About the bus stop. About my other body slumped against the locker. About all his friends smelling his fingers. About how he makes me want to unpin myself from myself.

You're so beautiful.

No one has ever called me that before and I know it can't be true. I don't know what he sees in front of him: a girl who's really a girl or what I am: a girl who's just pretending. I need a little space to think, I try to put my hand up between us, but it's in his wrist again. He's staring at me like he did that day at the terminal, like he'd let any bus go by to keep looking.

My body has unpinned itself again. And then re-pinned itself. It's unpinning and re-pinning so fast it's painful, so fast my head gets dizzy. His grip is so tight my fingers can't move, like he's afraid I'm going to disappear, like I'm going to fade right into myself.

Kareena doesn't say hi to me anymore. She just walks by me when I'm at my locker, her eyes deliberate and forward. I watch her long black braid disappear behind the bend of the hallway. I think of how I would have liked to be her friend.

I loved your mom,

Uncle ████ says, one summer night when he's around and trying to take care of us, prodding the chicken that is already burnt on the grill. Aisha's with her friends, Noreen at work. I'm about to be a junior, trying to decide how many AP classes I can take next year without getting overwhelmed. Oreo is by the window, watching us from inside.

Why did you all stop being close?

I ask as his hands turn the skewers, the small hairs on his fingers noticeable even from where I sit on my chair.

Sometimes the small things become the big things.

During the day, I'm watched, scheduled. But the night opens all its doors. I detangle myself from Aisha. Step over Noreen because she's home. Bobby is in his dad's car, waiting for me outside. I get in and make him close his eyes. I change into one of the dresses that Noreen brought home so long ago, one I couldn't normally leave the house in. A black one that stops halfway down my thighs, my bare knees huddled under to keep me warm. And he drives. We're so grown: juniors, a car, an apartment, legs out.

We're not together. Bobby is sometimes with Kareena, sometimes not. She still won't talk to me. He sometimes looks at me, sometimes doesn't. Tonight, he's next to me, driving, his eyes looking towards my thighs.

I don't think I've ever seen your legs.

We get there, where he wants to take me. A lake his dad took him to over the summer, a forty-minute drive from us. Tonight, it's just us, sneaking under the barricade. The water presses cold against our calves, calling us to come deeper.

We could spend all night on the grass with the moon hanging just there. We watch the lightning x-ray the sky. Bobby lays down next to me, on the thin blanket he brought. His hand reaches out for mine. I feel a spark of the fire in me, the embers beginning to heat. I look at his hand. He touches my leg with his fingers, and starts to move it up. The embers start to catch inside me. I need to put them out.

Hold on, I say, needing things to slow down. But he just smiles and continues to move his fingers up, touching the inside of my thigh.

I stand up. Walk to where the water meets the land. Mud under my toes. I'm so warm inside. I can't tell if I'm turned on or angry. I take off my dress, so I'm in my underwear and padded bra.

Hey, he says, and I feel him sit up even though I'm not next to him anymore. I don't look at him.

Everything is so hot. My body. My insides. I walk into the lake. The ripples in the water are soft. The water, mid-waist, smooth as a sheet. The flame inside me burns. My stinger rises behind me, splashing the water. I don't want him near. I could hurt him. And I don't want to.

What are you doing? he asks, his voice a few feet behind me. I don't turn but I can tell he's not on the blanket anymore, standing up.

Don't follow me, I say, my voice bossy, the stinger and heat making it strong, like it was the day in front of Uncle ████'s wife's house.

Bobby can't swim. He stays where the water hits his calves. I walk in deeper. Until my toes can't touch the sand. Until I float on my back.

Stop. I hear him. But he sounds a world away.

The water is so black it blends into the sky. The water laps my ears, the gift of fog. I can't hear him call my name. My insides are so hot; I sizzle in the water. Floating on my back out here like this, with the blackness all around me, I don't feel so lonely. My body stays in my body. There's nowhere else for it to go.

Bobby calls for me, but I'm having a conversation with the moon. It flickers from orange to pearl. I hear his voice when my ear rises above the water, it's gone when I dip back down. The lightning x-rays. Allah, let it reach the water, my body. Not him near the grass. Allah, keep him safe, somewhere far away from me. When my ears rise above the water I hear him. His voice is raw. His throat splintered. He calls my name. Calls and calls. My body shuts down in the coldness of the night, in the coldness of the water. My heartbeat pleads with me and wins.

It always wins. I drag my arms above me, cutting the darkness, my fingers thrashing into the still of the water. My heart beats: *alhumdulillah, alhumdulillah, alhumdulillah.* My insides are extinguished. My legs are too weak to move. I paddle my arms back to the land, shallow enough where I try to stand. He's in the water, dragging me out of her. I can feel the anger in his body, warming his skin.

What the fuck is wrong with you? he keeps saying, over and over.

Whatthefuckiswrongwithyou? The words slur together in my head.

We're on the blanket, his body draped over me like a sheet. I'm so cold I'm shaking, and his mouth is blowing warm air into my joints, just like Aunty used to do when she lived with us, when I lost my mittens and my hands got cold. His mouth is on my knee, on my thigh. His mouth on my hip, on my stomach. His mouth on my collarbone, on my neck. His mouth on my mouth. His tongue on my tongue.

Above me, the sky lightnings. A flame. Outside of me.

There is no God but God and from that God a million threads flow up from the earth. From that God grass grows. From that God we get trees. From that God, the moon. And that God threads all tiny cords to us useless humans, connecting to our navels like some long-forgotten invisible umbilical. All of us tethered by this light beam, some dingier than others, some so lost that they're coated in dust. Every time God breathes we feel a pull, some ghost lung that we convince ourselves isn't real.

I know he is no God, I know that there is no God but God. But when he moves I see the tether at his navel, so golden strong, so unbreakable. And I know that there has to be something special about him. A boy that golds. A boy with no doubt. Even if I don't want his fingers, even when my body tenses I tell myself to just relax, because there's so much light around him, so much dust around me.

I stand outside the apartment, still wet from the lake. I changed back into jeans and a T-shirt in the car, before Bobby dropped me off. He's on his way back home. I see dim lights on, a figure inside, watching me through the window. My hands break out with sweat beads. My chest is suddenly cold and clammy. My phone is dead in my pocket. All the missed calls, the warnings from Aisha and Noreen I'll never know.

When I turn the key to the apartment door, he's there. Uncle ███████, sitting on the couch. Noreen is pacing the living room floor. Aisha sits on the stool.

We're so watched. He always knows. Even though he's not there.

Where were you? he asks, his voice calm, but each syllable packed with venom.

My voice dies in my throat. He stands up. So still, it's eerie. My back presses against the wall.

Were you with a boy? Were you having sex?

His whole body crackles when he's angry. The electricity sparks off him. The cool calm as his fingers close around my throat, holding it to the door, pushing it into the wood. There's no wild thrashing about, just the concentration of his skin against my throat, robbing me of breath. My throat leaves my body, zooms out of me like a fly, watching from the wall. Its feet full of death. My sisters yell from the living room. Or maybe they're right next to me. Oreo darts into our room, afraid. Black spots fill my sight. Aisha's voice statics the whole apartment. My eyes focus on the part of the stove where the knob of the burner is supposed to be. It somehow got lost, accidentally brushed off by Aisha or me, both of us too lazy to look for it. It's something we should find, really, so that we don't have to keep turning the steel nail and hoping the thing lights. Noreen's on the phone, screaming for help. The sirens come. His hands move off me. I fall to the floor, my knees hit the tile. My eyes in line with his shoes. He looks down at me, his hands slip so easily back into his pockets. He turns and goes to open the door for the police.

Who are they going to believe?

[   ] or [   ]?

[you].

Them: Did he hurt you?

Me: ██

Them: We got a call and we're just trying to understand what
happened. Could you tell us?

Me: ██

Them: Is your Uncle your legal guardian?

Me: ██

Them: Does your Uncle live with you?

Me: ██

Them: Do you have other family?

Me: ██

Them: So, is your sister making this up?

Me: ██

We're in the same room, but Noreen is so far away I can't touch her. Uncle ███████ has pulled all of the phone lines out of the walls. Canceled our cellphone plans. The disconnect rings. No one can reach us. We can't call out.

Why did you lie? she asks and my voice dries.

Desert throat. Sand voice. Fly on the wall.

And then gentler, questioning: *Did I make it up?* Her eyes furrow. *Is it not as bad as it seems?*

I look around our apartment. The fridge, full of chicken breasts and grilled vegetables. Soy milk and applesauce. Oreo sits on the couch in a patch of sun.

It's fine. We're doing fine, I say, my voice mine and not mine, my voice coming from another me inside myself.

I reach towards Noreen, but she pulls away. Her unfocused eyes stare out the window, which is shoe level with the street. People walk by us. In their own worlds. She's in her own world, her eyes not the eyes I know but another Noreen's. She turns her back on me. Her shoulders shrink into herself. We're all shrinking into ourselves. Practicing how small we can be. If I close my eyes and will it, I can become the air. I can disappear entirely.

There is a me who watches from above, tucked into the corner where the wall meets the ceiling. My skin skies the apartment. I'm there, watching my me below trying to reach Noreen. My me below, full of me-shaped holes. Split. Splitting more with each passing second. All my me's pour out of my main me. My main me bleeds me's. My main me too torn to even notice.

You sneak back in okay?
Yes.

I keep thinking about your legs.
Mhmm.

When are we going to the lake again?
I dunno.

I knocked the fuck out. I didn't do none of my homework, I think
Ms. Adams is gonna be mad at me.
I can help you.

I open a can of tuna and spread it out on crackers, dinner the night after the police officers came. Aisha lounges on the couch, her foot on the crook of the window. Oreo sits at my feet, eyes on me, wanting the tuna. Noreen looks at the counter in disgust, blinking slowly.

I hate living like this, Noreen confesses. Aisha doesn't even stir from where she sits.

It's not that bad. We're all fine, I say and Noreen looks up at me, her eyes ice.

(I want to know.)(What you mean.)(When you say.)

(I want you to know.)(What I mean.)(When I say.)

It's fine. I'm fine. We're all fine.

A word is a word is a word.

Sister;
Noreen, sitting so far away from me I can't touch her.
Aisha, in her own world, taking on extra shifts to get us food.

Sister;
A thousand hearts light up the sky.
A thousand different hearts dampen.

Mother;
And here they come, all our mothers
a tower or a warm meal

                         depending.

The age-old question:
Is an apple always an apple?
Is an apple an apple when someone's taken a bite out of it?
Is a sister still a sister when a mother dies?

Allah asked us to make language. And so we did. Named all our parts. Named the blue inside us. The heartbreak. The love. Then, we forgot about him. Our language became cement. It settled. Tower. Babel. The fall. The lightning struck. Our throats changed. We separated. We assumed we meant the same thing when we spoke, because we said the same words. But. We were wrong. We were so wrong.

A few nights later, I detangle myself from Aisha's arms. I slip out past her, so tired that an earthquake wouldn't disturb her from sleep. My anger blood hot. My anger laces up my shoes, and walks me to the PATH station. I wait in the dead of night for buses to come, for me to make the transfers. It's just me, my anger, the driver, and the slow blinking lights. My anger carries me across the suburban yards where they live. I've only been once, but I remember. When she slammed the door in our faces, his sons watching, the other side of our partition. Their lush house, the garden outside small, but flowered. Watered with my dead father's money.

My chest is too cold for the spring night around me. *He was never yours to begin with,* I say to myself, closing my eyes to remember. The way his real family surrounded him at the funeral, us watching from miles away through the TV screen. The way Uncle █████ never mentions him. How a stranger could take him from us in the middle of the night. I breathe out and feel my body separate from itself. I watch my other self look at me, angry. She has my face, my body, my soft snarl that I've adopted from Noreen. Her hair wild, her curls out, where mine is straightened with an iron, pulled back into a ponytail. She is the me who wants justice. The me who wants what could have been mine. The me who wants that man to still be alive so she can show up at his doorstep. The me who would say, *you killed my father.* The me who would have a knife in her back pocket. An eye for an eye. A life for a life. The me who is standing outside this suburban house. The me who knows the money that's paying for it. The me who wants to torch their whole house, cut up all their designer clothes. Scorpion sting and venom. Making everything a desert. The me who wants my father back. And if not him, at least his money.

She's there, watching the house. That me. I need help. I turn my back and leave her there, running when she calls my name, running when she begs me to not leave her behind, running as the fear in her voice rises.

At the doctor's office, my diagnosis is that I'm hairy. Uncle ▮▮▮▮▮ made me come here after the night he couldn't find me. But here I am, not pregnant. Still a virgin. Just hairy. *Like Frida Kahlo*, the pediatrician says, not turning around to look at me, typing the results into her computer. *She was an artist. She had a unibrow.* The hairs between my eyebrows sit up, at attention, at the mention of their brethren on someone else's face. How did this Frida person allow hers to live? To flourish. To be a part of her.

You have too much testosterone. It's an imbalance. You could try birth control to tame it, she suggests. *It has estrogen in it.*

If I feed my body estrogen I can become closer to being a woman. The hair on my fingers, the hair trailing up my arms, the hair above my upper lip and my goatee all quake, their demise imminent. I am a body full of hair, a little monster that lurks the hallways of my school. When I walk I feel everyone's eyes on me, looking at it. I don't even know if I want to look more like a woman. I just want people to stop staring at me. I try Nair, which smells like plastic burning when I lather it on my skin. But the Nair won't get rid of all of it, I spread and spread, wipe and wipe, only some of the hair coming off at a time. My legs red, raw, and stinging.

———

They look like undercooked chicken, Aisha says, not even trying to be mean, just concerned.

Our bathtub is always clogged, when I shower the water pools up to my ankles. When I shave, the water is still there, filled with black curls and soap suds. Aisha yells at me half an hour later when she sees I didn't clean it and calls me useless. My little hairs cling to the tub for dear life. I pile them up in the center of the tub, the massacre in exchange for two days of smooth. They eventually grow back, thicker, unrelenting, and the process repeats again and again. Aisha's yell on loop. They're everywhere, nestled between the corner tiles of the bathroom, somehow littered across the sink. The patch I missed behind my ankle noticeable in the sunlight as I walk from the bus station to school. I try and rid myself of them and they keep finding their way back.

Yes, you are hairy, Uncle ▇▇▇ says as I confront him with
the enormity of my problem. *Both of you are,* he adds, his eyes
moving from me to Aisha. The two of us fur balls, always fighting. Hairy. Picked over. Rough around the edges. Hard to
marry off. He goes to the computer and clicks and clicks, finding a site that sells discount drugs from Mexico. He bulk-
orders packs of birth control, off-brand and international.

How can he order drugs across borders? I whisper, but Aisha
shakes her head and we both get quiet.

We don't care how as long as we get them. The rule: Don't ask
questions. You get what you get.

It'll be enough to last you a year, he beams, getting up from the
table, putting his jacket on.

A gold star of parenting suddenly fastened over the hole in his
sweater.

Victoria and I haven't spoken in weeks. She's mad, saying I've forgotten about her, but I don't know how to say that I'm tired all the time, dragging my body around like a sack. We fight on the phone, the scorpion in me flicks its stinger. *You don't even care about me, you don't even know what I'm going through. You're not a fucking friend,* I say, knowing damn well how deliberately I've tried to hide what I'm going through. Uncle ███ sits with his back turned towards me, using our computer, clicking away. When I hang up, he asks me to go for a drive with him.

It's silent in the car. I look out the window until he turns down a road and stops in front of Victoria's house.

Don't let the small things become the big things.

Kareena's long braid swings behind her as she walks. In the morning she sits on the wall outside of school with her friends, her clear backpack boasting Revlon eyeliner, a pink notebook, and her TI-89. The sun peeks through the leaves just to be able to get to her. Every time she laughs the dimples spread across her cheeks. In class, when she's thinking, her jaw tightens, the veins in her neck move a little, each one carrying her heartbeat through her. But it doesn't look strained, like the boys in gym when they're showing off. It looks so delicate, her veins, her breath, everything about her so light she looks like she might not be real at all. When she's around, I can't stop looking at her, memorizing her perfectly glossed lips, her cat-eyes winged to the heavens.

When Bobby finds me in the hallway or after school I imagine Kareena's fingers instead, Kareena's perfect mouth on mine. And my body morphs, more muscular, I grow taller, my breasts dissolve back into my chest. For this girl, I can be whatever shape she needs me to be, whatever shape makes the veins in her neck go, whatever reminds her that her heart is still beating.

In the morning, Kareena passes me in the hall and doesn't say anything. But her ghost dimples stay with me all day, her long black braid swinging in my periphery. Every time I turn to look for it, it's gone, she's gone, she was never there. But I carry her with me, I carry her into our apartment, I keep her in my pocket, and when Aisha sleeps over at a friend's house, when I'm sure I'm alone, I take her out and watch her as my fingers come alive.

After school the whole world watches Bobby weaving on the court, shoes squeaking against the wood. The bleachers bow, the net calls his name. He's perfectly framed: the gymnasium lights kissing his face, finding their way to him. All around him flies careen, all around the world buzzes at his brightness.

I don't know why he looks at me the way he does. Why after every shot he makes he looks up and smiles at me. Why he finds me after school, his fingers on my skin. When he puts his hands across my body now I don't flinch, I stay perfectly still, because being his feels better than being alone. When I walk without him, the other girls look me up and down. *She's not even that pretty.* And I'm not even a little bit pretty, so it doesn't feel like an insult.

After the game, he says he's going to walk me home. All his boys file out of the locker room. I wait for him on the bleachers. The boys say bye to me as they leave. They're all being so nice. He's the last one out, he walks over to me. Even a year of him sometimes being around and sometimes not, my knees still have a hard time remembering how to stand when he shows up.

For him, I make myself a girl. Not perfect, but: a girl. I try to picture him walking through our one-bedroom apartment. I try to imagine him sitting on our trundle bed with me. I try to imagine us scouring the fridge together for what we can make into a meal before we curl up on the couch.

It's okay, you don't have to walk me.

But his arm is around my waist, pulling me close to him, and my stupid knees can't hold their ground. All around me the air is made of him, and I can't get away from it. We're alone outside the gym and his hand is going up my jacket. His hand is in my waistband, digging into my hip. I flinch on accident, and for a second, I see a flash of confusion cross his eyes. I feel bad. I understand how difficult I am, all my awkward bones, my inability to relax.

But I want to meet your parents.

Sometimes he looks at me like I'm a tender precious thing on the brink of break. He says *my heart*, and maybe that's what his hand is, maybe that's what my hand is when they touch, a pulse that keeps me tethered to the ground. And maybe that's what his hand is when it slips inside me, maybe it's just his heart trying to find my heart, trying to touch it.

Tonight, after our walk, we stand in the living room of my tiny apartment, in the middle of my garbage pile. My anxiety is high, Uncle ███ told us he was going out of town, but I'm afraid he might magically appear out of nowhere. That he has eyes everywhere. That his hand will be around my neck again. But I risk it, to have Bobby in my living room. To have him looking at me the way he is.

So this is why you didn't want to go home that day.

His eyebrows furrow, he looks towards the window, to the blue Cadillac that I had pointed out to him, ███'s. This small one-bedroom apartment, that blue Cadillac. He's trying to do the math. But the math doesn't make sense. The space between us multiplies, and I know that I'm going to lose his hand in my hand.

———

But he wraps his arms around me, holding me, both anchor and bench. His eyes on my eyes. Soft. Gentle. Like the day at the bus station. The embarrassment of my world all around, and him: unembarrassed, drinking it in.

Aisha is already in bed, wrestling in her sleep, battling in her silent world. Noreen is there too, she's been coming home more since the night with the police. They're separated from me and Bobby by the bit of fabric that hangs. Roaches scurry across the floor, our presence intrudes on their night freedom. We sit on the worn-down couch. His eyes move from the Nilla Wafers package to the mouse trap.

When he's here, in my world, he's not the star of the court. His eyes are so soft, like he knows the cost of touching me. Watching him right now, I know what it means to have my heart outside my body, to have my heart in someone else.

I lay down on the couch, and he lays down next to me, my black hair on his chest. He told me his mom won't care if he doesn't come home and I wonder what it's like to have a mom who loves you but lets you belong to the night, who lets you belong to a maybe-girl she's never met.

Where are they?

I don't have to ask to know who he wants to know about. My parents of the make-believe, my dad with the name of a king, my mom with her piano fingers.

They're gone.

I think Allah stopped watching me a long time ago but I'm afraid what else he might take from me if I continue to mess up, if I continue to be a useless fly on his earth, buzzing around my pile of garbage. I don't want to go to hell. We can move in silence and maybe Allah will look the other way. *Allah, forgive me for being janky,* I think in my head, Bobby's eyes on my lips. When his fingers slip inside me this time, on the couch, I don't unpin from myself. I hear my breath become a different breath, a longer breath, a breath of my skin rather than my lungs. His fingers are outside of me but something larger is pressing in, and my teeth are biting down on his shoulder to stop the pain, to stay in silence, and he's moving fast, and he buries his face in the couch pillow to stop the sound, and I can feel everything this time, and even though there are so many holes in my body—so many other me's—my body doesn't leave my body to watch, my body finally stays.

Can you make it last?

I whisper into his chest as he sleeps and he stirs slightly, his eyebrows creasing at his forehead.

This feeling. Can you make it last?

In the morning, when we are both awake, he wants to stay awhile but he has a mother to get back to. My sisters don't leave the bedroom but whisper from behind the curtain.

There are no adults, so there's no need for him to crawl out the window. From the window I watch him leave, fade into the daylight. My grief hasn't touched him, hasn't ruined him yet.

Aisha walks out of the room, arms crossed, pissed. Noreen following her.

Who is he?
Are you fucking?
Are you dating?
You brought him here?
We lied to Uncle ████ *for you.*

I thought I knew the rules, but apparently, I've broken one.

Aisha blinks slow and hard, arms crossed, looking at me like she can't quite believe that I exist. Noreen's tongue pressed lightly behind her two front teeth, like she's looking at me for the first time.

Do you love him?

————

And asked like that, the question sounds stupid, hanging in the air, taking up space. An accusation. My sisters' eyes on me and it's all laid out, so plain, so simple, I wonder how I didn't see it before.

You're my heart too.

And I need them to know this, how, long ago, I put my heart inside their hearts. How I was born this way, belonging to them, trying to follow their breath. How I've given them each a slice of it, how there isn't any of my own heart in my own body, how close I am to breaking all the time.

Aisha's forehead storms again. She clenches her fists and her thin veins light up. And Noreen's lips curve down, her fingers digging into her arms, creating soft red crescent moons on her skin. We stare at each other, all together, the first time in what feels like years. Eyes moving, brown to brown to brown. This time, no one laughs.

The three of us, on an island, alone. A dying fire and no rescue in sight. The three of us crouch on the beach, baring our teeth. The three of us circle each other, sniffing out our fear, wondering who is fit for survival. Which one of us bleeds? Which one of us drew blood? I'm a not-girl full of holes, all my me's run away into the wild. All my mes' skin hanging from the trees, flayed, as they split off into more and more me's. They're gone and I don't know if I'm ever going to get them back. I don't know if I want to. The trees turn away from us in shame. One of us charges forward, attacking. I don't know where my skin ends and my sister-mothers' begins.

A week later, when it's just me and Aisha, she speaks so quietly her voice almost blends into her blanket, muffled by cotton.

Do you think she thinks she's better than us?

She doesn't need to say who she's talking about. I know. The trundle bed is empty. In the darkness of our room, you can't see the photo of Meemoo and Aunty I've put up on the wall. It covers the roach Aisha smushed with her chapal, its guts we never bothered to clean off. Noreen is gone, at school. Spending longer and longer chunks of time away from us. Even though she is gone, Aisha and I still sleep in the same twin bed in case she comes back. My fingers trace the wrinkles in our sheets, I can't remember the last time we washed them. Our washing machine is always broken and when it works, there are always more important things that need to be washed, like underwear or jeans.

No. She said she'll come back Friday.

Aisha sighs, my answer stupid and not good enough. I can't see her face but I know her eyebrows are slightly furrowed, thinking.

———

We're supposed to be a family.

Her voice gets caught in the blanket. I feel her armor, I feel her start to slip into her world where I can't follow.

Aisha at school, surrounded by all the friends she loves. Aisha, at home, on the island alone. Turning to stone. Swim practice in the morning before school. School. Then home after work at the T.J. Maxx. Days and days of work, days and days of school, days and days of swim practice, days and days of eating PowerBars we got weeks ago from Costco and pretending it's a real meal. No food in the fridge. In the twin bed, the fabric curtain distorting the shapes outside. All around, the storm threatens to come in, the rain flooding the soil. A wolf, in search of food. She gets up, tries to prowl, her legs weak. She scours the cabinets, the blood rushing to her head. A black dot blinking in her sight. The walls are thin, beyond them the laundry machine thumps loudly. Oreo meows in the living room. She calls for help but no one is around to answer. She turns on the faucet, glass in hand, and there's a stream of yellowish water. She waits for it to clear.

Aisha is in the kitchen, a wolf alone. Me, down the street at the bus stop, waiting for Noreen. Friday, just like she said. There are more black dots. Like film gone bad. They creep and creep. Aisha's body breaks into bumps. The water is still yellow. The glass in her hand shakes.

The dots take over. Until there are only dots. Until there's only dizzy. She blinks into the darkness and all she sees is dark.

———

Her legs slack, her head smacks the counter, the glass falls from her hand, her body falls onto the floor. Blood draws. From her head where it hit the counter. From her hand, the glass she was holding. A wolf alone. A wolf, hurt. The faucet still sputtering yellow.

Noreen and I come home, at the tail end of the storm, and there she is: Aisha. No one else home but Oreo. The red spreading from her head, from the cut in her hand.

—a pool of rose. My heart hammers and hammers. Spilled ketchup. Wine on the floor. Rooh Afza, sticky, syrupy sweet. Stretching, stretching, stretching. The smell of the butcher shop. A spill of my heart on the floor. Aisha in a river of her own. The cut on her head shallow enough to keep most of her blood in her body. Alhumdulillah. Aisha's eyes unfocused. My eyes unfocus. My knees unfocus. My knees, dots on the floor. My breath loud in my ears. All I can hear is my own breath, Noreen's feet running forward, Noreen's yell, the beat of my heart, Aisha's heart, pounding—

Noreen presses an old dishrag to Aisha's head, stilling the blood. Noreen says something to Aisha, Aisha says something back. There's a ringing in my ears. Everything far away. Everything too close. The blood still on the floor. Noreen calls Uncle ██████. He doesn't answer. Aisha, holding the dishrag in place with one hand, calls a friend of hers with a car. We wait. Aisha's head leaning back against the cabinet. Her eyes closed. Her head tilted up.

Next to me, another me rips out of my skin. She sits, watching the blood. Her eyes fixed on the red.

When they left to go to the hospital, I stayed at home and threw up in a plastic takeout bag. My head full of dots. My knees unfocused. The blood still on the floor. Noreen called Uncle ███████ over and over. Aisha, blood sticky in her hair, called too. He did not come. He answered the phone once, heard her voice bleat, and hung up. She called him back, the missed calls piling up. He's nowhere to be found. He must be with his sons at some event, where everyone is dressed in fancy salwars and kameezes, where everyone is freshly washed and smells like jasmine. He must be somewhere else, cracking a smile as he greets a stranger while his sister's daughters are alone in a one-bedroom apartment, fainting, the towels soaking up the blood. Oreo pawing the door. Aisha's unfocused eyes. A new fear burrows at the pit of my throat: that Aisha can be gone at any moment too. Aisha's or Noreen's blood, all over the floor. They can leave, by accident, just like Meemoo and Aunty. Just like our parents. The space inside my chest multiplies. Us in the apartment, alone. Us, alone from each other.

When he resurfaces from his silence, Uncle ███████ pretends like nothing happened. He buys Aisha a fake Louis Vuitton purse she'll never use and the last Harry Potter book and doesn't mention the blood. Doesn't mention the missed calls. Doesn't mention the hospital. We don't either.

You have to learn to drive, he says.

I go with him on chicken runs through the neighborhoods. He shows me a megaphone he got from the Home Depot before rolling down the passenger-side window. He blares out the street-cleaning schedule to anyone who is around, minding their own business. The older South Asian people wait outside their houses and we stop in front, me at the wheel. He opens the trunk to reveal iceboxes full of frozen chicken. *Discounted prices!* he yells and people fumble for cash in their pockets, handing it over to him. From the rearview mirror I watch as he counts the money carefully. He bubbles over in his excitement, his jubilation at this new scheme he's acquired. *No, bhai, don't worry about it, you could pay me next week,* he says, joyfully slapping an Uncle on the shoulder. The man smiles back, gap-toothed. However nothing Uncle ███████ offers comes for free. I know that, but the man does not. I watch him carry his chicken back to his apartment, balancing his hand on the railing as he slowly pushes himself up the porch stairs. I play *Pon de Replay* from the car, it spills onto the sidewalk. Uncle

███ dances outside, his shoulders moving bhangra-style and not entirely to the beat. The neighbors laugh, and I'm struck by how normal this all seems: an Uncle and his niece, a chicken run, about to drive back to an apartment where no one questions what happens inside.

We switch seats—him back in the driver's seat. He hands me a crisp twenty-dollar bill.

You're easier to be around than your sisters, he says, looking over at me, his eyes warm.

Yeah, they're difficult, I say, staring out the window at a tree trying to thrive in the sidewalk.

Them: So, is your sister making this up?

Me: ■

I left when I was nine,

Uncle ██████ says from behind the wheel, unprompted, as if we're mid-conversation.

The British left. They called it Partition. They drew the new countries. But so many of us, we'd lived where we lived. Our families, next to each other. The lines, telling us to go, telling us our new countries, they didn't mean anything. But there were men, our neighbors, looking for Muslims. We were Muslim, we were on the wrong side of the line.

The light turns green, but he keeps the car still. A car honks, but he does not move. The car skids around him, into the next lane.

There were houses, burning. My ammi, your nanni, told me to pack. I was so young. I didn't know what to bring. I filled a suitcase with my toys. We got on a train. And when the train stopped, there was a field. A field of bodies. Dead, Muslim bodies.

Another car honks, swerves around us. A white man sends up his middle finger at Uncle ██████. But he stares straight ahead at the road, not moving.

———

I remember the flies. The ground was so wet. They were piling bodies on top of each other.

He fiddles with the radio dial but no sound comes out.

Your ammi was so young then. A baby. My little sister. I carried her. Her cheeks were so round. She kept looking at me. Everyone was screaming all around us. And she kept looking at me. We got split up from my father. I tried to look back and find him but I couldn't. We ran through the field. Through a forest. I never saw my father again.

Another car honks, another car drives past.

They killed so many of the Muslims who stayed. Sometimes it's better to keep things separate. When they don't belong together. When you mix them, bad things can happen.

The light turns red. My Uncle's hand moves back to the wheel.

That's why we left. That's why we went to Pakistan.

He puts his foot on the gas. He runs the light. We leave the red behind.

Noreen's outside pacing when we pull up, Oreo on a leash. So much space between me and Aisha. So much space between me and Noreen. I want to be somewhere else. I want a different pile of garbage to sort through. I open the car door and hesitate before shutting it. *Bye, beti*, he says and smiles. I smile back. He leaves us standing there on the sidewalk. *Why are you smiling?* she asks and my smile disappears into the wind. *Beti*, she imitates him, and it sounds like a curse. *Don't tell me you actually like spending time with that piece of shit.*

I'm fine, Aisha says, lying on the twin bed. *Stop looking at me.* They put a big Band-Aid on her head at the hospital, said she needed a lot of rest but she'd be fine eventually. Oreo on her stomach, his purr loud.

Aisha's fingers play with her hair, finding a tangle. She pulls hard, the rip breaks the silence of the room. Noreen's meal-plan food in our fridge. Noreen back at school.

It's not like you did anything anyway, she says, a dark laugh in her throat.

Useless, she sighs, turning away. My chest gets sticky inside. The blood on the floor. My knees going weak. All the dots in my body. My other me, still there, watching.

Useless
/ˈyo͞osləs/
Adjective;

The drain in our bathtub, clogged with all our hair. The way it won't let the water down unless we bend a wire hanger and scrape a lifetime of our cells out. The stale bathwater that rises past our ankles every time we take a shower, no matter how short. Empty bottles in the trash can. The busted microwave in the kitchen. The always-empty fridge. My sticky locker at school. My student bus card on the weekends. The dirty snow piled on the side of the road. Flat soda that takes up space in the fridge. A paper towel when trying to get blood out of the floor.

I stand at the edge of the door to our bathroom and open it, and my grief greets me. Who is out there? The Past, a black hole, roaring. It swirls and swirls, I feel its center trying to pull me in. My grief calls to me, and it's loud. The only God I can hear. Begging me to not forget. Everything is stuck inside it: my dead father, my dead mother, the countries they came from that I don't know. Meemoo. Aunty. A night of a thousand moons, all upside down, hanging like streetlights. A dark sky, silver fish swimming in its upstream, a river of stars. The black hole pulls my father's face wide, his smile cheshiring, wrapping teeth all around me. Then he collapses into nothingness, his fingers ghosting into space. The night peels off into night. I close my eyes and call to the God of death, to whatever God might help me. *Please,* I beg, and my grief yells my name, asks me to come to it. Its shadow braids into my shadow, I cast it wherever I stand.

I get pulled out of third-period English to my guidance counselor's office. She's at the computer, looking over my credits.

You're smart, she says, glancing over her shoulder at me.

Smart enough to graduate early if you wanted.

I tap my shoe on the ground. I never considered it before, leaving early. Aisha's going to college soon. Noreen is already gone. Bobby is playing a game tonight. He asked me to come. She clicks a few keys on her computer and the printer starts. We watch the paper come out and she slides it towards me.

Do you want to? You would need to take this home and have your parents sign it.

As though I need a parent to permission anything. All those years ago, sitting at the table, watching Noreen and Aisha learning to forge Uncle ███████'s signature. I take the paper and leave.

During the game, Bobby's mother sits in the bleachers. His dad is at work, but left him a voicemail saying he was proud of him. I sit across the gym from his mom, the lids underneath my eyes making them dark. She got off work to see him play. His little brother sits next to her. Everyone knows she is his mom, everyone smiles at her and says *hello Mrs. Perez* and the corners of her eyes break into a river of wrinkles. Around her, a ring of light that matches his. I see where he gets it from. Tonight is his night: he runs back and forth and no one can touch him, he slips through everyone's fingers, rising so high his chest is practically bursting. Every time he shoots he searches the audience for her face, as if asking *is she watching, did she see me*, but her eyes never move from him, not for one second.

I sit on the cracked toilet bowl and pray for my body to not make red, to tell me there's another body inside mine. Something that connects me to him. *I have another heart for you.* Droplets of piss sprinkle the floor, the lights flicker in and out above me as I pray. I hear the new couple fight in Omar's old apartment. Their Urdu is muffled so I can't make out the words. I think of Bobby, a mirror of his mother's light, a mirror of her eyes river-ing on the bleachers. He reflects and reflects, and the world around him becomes his image. He belongs to the world, when he runs the world sings *that's my heart right there.* When I went up to meet his mom after the game he held my wrist hard. I knew that meant *no.* I sat on the bleachers and watched his whole team hug her, watched Kareena with her long braid tied neatly in a ribbon smile sweetly. His mom held Kareena's hands in hers. And there they were: Bobby and Kareena, all dimples, what could have been mine. I sat on the bleachers until the whole court emptied, until Mr. Stevenson came along with the broom and said that I had to go home so he could turn off the lights. And now, the test tells me that there's nothing inside me, that after all, that after everything, I'm alone.

It's not even like we were anything, you know? We just hung out a few times.
If you say so.

You get it, right? Like, I like you, but Kareena, that's my girl.
Okay.

I feel like you're getting sensitive about it and I didn't do any-thing wrong.
Sorry.

You didn't do anything wrong.

I wake to Aisha running her fingers through my hair. She grazes her nails along my scalp. Like how she used to run them across the cello. Tender. Aisha is here, now, next to me. Her breath gentle. Home from a long day and still making time for me. Sensing something is wrong, but letting me keep my quiet about it. In a few months, she'll be in college. I'll be in this apartment alone. Uncle ███████ will be here sometimes. And sometimes he won't. The paper is in my bag. I know how to sign his name. But right now, it's Aisha and me in this twin bed. She's playing with my hair. And I don't know how, but I know she knows.

In the morning, before school starts, he's at the wall again, his arm gently around Kareena. She's all eyes on him, the golden cross resting perfectly between her collarbones. The smile on his face looks like she's transferred her dimples to him. He's looking at her like he's never looked at anyone else, like no one else exists. When the bell rings and everyone gets ready to go to class, he takes Kareena's hand, her long black braid swinging, and I hear him turn to his boys and say *this, this my heart right here.*

Noreen comes home from school and I can't tell if it's Noreen or not. Her eyes are hazy, she can't keep focused on anything. Her skin doesn't pearl like usual, it dips into a gray-blue undertone I've never seen before. Noreen won't look at me or Aisha, won't speak to us, just sleeps. A Sleeping Beauty, perhaps, except this Noreen is not beautiful, this Noreen doesn't look like my Noreen, this Noreen looks like a stranger. Aisha leaves to get water, and I sit on the edge of her trundle. And before I realize what I am doing, before I can help myself, my fingers graze her ankle just slightly, drawing a pattern on her skin.

My little radiator.

And for a moment, she's back. Noreen, my God. God of the Dollar Store Lipstick. God of the Raspy Voice.

Noreen is lying down, smiling up at me, as though nothing has happened. The Noreen from before college. The Noreen from before the call to the police.

You left us. Before I can stop myself, the words are out of my mouth, the words a dagger that shapes midair towards her.

So did you, bitch.

———

Aisha comes back with the glass of water and Noreen is asleep again. When the quiet comes, when it settles over us, I know: she's right.

Bobby's fingers thread through Kareena's long braid. The missed calls to Uncle ████. Noreen's smudged lipstick, the lilt of her voice. Useless. The empty hallway. The birds gone. A murdered father. An already-dead killer. The dull flame inside me. Forgive and forget. Meemoo and Aunty gone. Noreen wanting anyone but us. Aisha going to college in a few months. No one to ever help. No one to answer the phone. The paper in my bag. Graduating early. His laugh in the lunchroom. His fingers inside me. My body split. My love, pretend. Me, pretending to be a girl for him. Me, not a girl. Me, not a boy. My tether to two misshapen bodies. How there's never any food. Strangers howling into the night. Him on the basketball court and the crowd beaming. His mother in the stands. I can't remember my mother's face. Out of all the strangers, she's the strangest.

How terrible—to be an ordinary orphan. Not a superhero. Not a wizard in waiting. Not a prophet who goes to a cave. Just—ordinary. All that grief, wasted. All that fucking grief for nothing.

I stand above Noreen and Aisha as they sleep on the twin bed and trundle. They look so perfect right now, two girls that could be napping in a dorm room. The air in their chests, moving in and out.

I can't live like this.

I hold the bus ticket in my hand. All the Gods that live in the night sky blink down to us through the fog of the city. The one God I bend my knees to. The suitcase is tucked beneath my legs as I sit on a bench at the station. If I go somewhere new, I can start over. History doesn't need to know my name. My stupid pain. All the places I've left myself. What can't be fixed. I could belong to everything. I could build my home in nowhere.

her

he's a stupid man, always
concerned with the wrong thing.
my husband: the aspiring doctor, obsessed
with the idea that love can be proven
through things

in front of me now, the dream
in his eyes fading. the machine's song
humming the background, the hospital
light unflattering, my hair gone
the tubes up my nose

i can't believe
he brought them—my children.

he's a stupid man, sentimental
thinking this is important for them
to see. by this, i mean me dying.

by see, i mean how their sight
sights the ceiling, the hospital bed
the machine, how they burrow their
little faces into their baba & ask
to go home

i could never
figure out what
to give you.

my husband, eyelashes
like spider legs
wet, breath caught
rattling his chest

too young, with a dead wife
too young, a bunch of kids
tugging on him
like he knows what to do

they're all I wanted

my gifts, too young
to be in this room

my gifts, eyes on anything
but me

his eyes come back to mine
& we're young again, alive
at our wedding, the mirror between us
when my eyes see his
for the first time

mashallahs
on everyone's lips

we're young again
that first apartment
the mattress on the floor
so bare

the fridge emptied
but for his laugh, which
warmed, which honeyed me

his fingers goosebumping
my skin, his lick lullabying
me to sleep

now, at the end of it all
his fear, that i married him
& my life ended

that it wasn't good

a stupid boy, measuring
love in the wrong things

                              there's one last gift
                                       i want

his spider lashes turn to me
desperate, the web
he'd cast. anything. he'd do.
anything.

the hospital door opens, real doctors
rush in. not my husband, aspiring
not my husband, sticky with hope

                         love them. love them hard.
                           keep them close. make
                            them love each other.

there: his beautiful, stupid
eyes look at me, lost
as always.

meri jaan.

& he nods, the promise made.

                                        say goodbye to your mother.

none of my children move.
goodbye, my angels

goodbye.

Sister. Sister. Sister. Sister. Sister.
Sister. Sister. Sister. Sister. Sister.
Sister. Sister. Sister. Sister. Sister.
Sister. Sister. Sister. Sister. Sister.
Sister. Sister. Sister. Sister. Sister.
Sister. Sister. Sister. Sister. Sister.
Sister. Sister. Sister. Sister. Sister.
Sister. Sister. Sister. Sister. Sister.
Sister. Sister. Sister. Sister. Sister.
Sister. Sister. Sister. Sister. Sister.
Sister. Sister. Sister. Sister. Sister.
Sister. Sister. Sister. Sister. Sister.
Sister. Sister. Sister. Sister. Sister.
Sister. Sister. Sister. Sister. Sister.
Sister. Sister. Sister. Sister. Sister.
Sister. Sister. Sister. Sister. Sister.
Sister. Sister. Sister. Sister. Sister.

Allah, I prayed for space & you answered with a whole galaxy. I thought you forgot me. But you always answer. I'm of my own planet, aloned. I look for my sisters. For my suns. I wake & my hands stay cold.

mer__ dil

reasons why people go—

When Uncle ███ dies I don't find out through a phone call
or a letter. I don't know why I thought it would come in a letter, an invitation to his funeral, the same way an invite to a
wedding comes in the mail. Not that anyone has my address—
I move too much for anyone to keep track of me. Sometimes I
find myself wandering to old apartments that I lived in before,
I watch the new people going about their lives as though they've
always been there. Sometimes I find myself going back to old
loves only to catch them with new loves—girlfriends, boy-
friends, theyfriends—moving forward as though I was just a
small blip on their radar. Just a small sentence in their story.

I'm twenty-seven now and when I move into a new apartment
I still live as if I might leave at any moment—my stuff in the
suitcases, furniture I find on the street cobbled together into a
makeshift home. I can make anything out of nothing, and I
can make it last through the night, and the next night, and the
night after that. Living like that—night by night—is what
gets me through all my nights, is what makes my years on this
earth a compilation of one lonely night after another, though I
never really sleep alone.

On the night I get the news that my Uncle has died, there's a
new someone in my apartment, smoking a blunt by the open

window. A new him in a long line of thems. Sometimes they are shes. Sometimes theys. My whole world brimming with thems, with the theys who touch me, with the theys who smile at me when I walk down the street, with the theys who promise to call me back and never do. I don't say much, but I fall in love with all of them.

Before him I dated someone who reminded me of Kareena. She didn't look like her at all. But the same gentleness. Voice warm. Friendly to everyone. We worked together and I would crash on her couch at night. Started fucking each other. Learned how to strap. Felt like what it would be like to have a dick as a part of me. Honestly, my stroke game probably could've been better. But I pretended like I was the best to ever fuck. Fake it until you make it, or whatever they say. We fell into dating. So slow I didn't even realize what was happening until she said, *bitch we're dating*, and I realized yes, that was in fact what we were doing. *Why don't you know how to date?* she'd ask, joking, but also, not. At restaurants we would write a list of countries we wanted to visit together on tablecloths. She got annoyed though, said I was too withdrawn. That she could never tell what I was thinking. She wanted me to talk more. Which made me talk less. And then I left, moved to this new apartment without her, and we never went to any of those countries. All the people I've dated blur into each other. They never leave. They mess in my dreams into a soup of faces.

I get a text from a number that I don't recognize, almost delete it without opening it. But something stops me. And when I click on it, Noreen's name is there, like she knew that I would have done something to forget about her, deleted her number, or else—never saved it: *its noreen. uncle* ▮▮▮▮ *died. cancer or some shit. funerals tomorrow.* All lowercase, no sorrow, disease or death or some other inconvenience.

And for a second my heart stops, not because my Uncle is dead but because I've seen her name, a name that used to be my sun, for the first time in years. *Inna lillahi wa inna ilayhi raji'un,* I type back.

To Him we belong, to Him we return.

My Uncle died, I say to the coffee table that I found three blocks away, that was too heavy for me to carry by myself but that I did anyway, hurting my back. The coffee table that has the old water glass stains on it from another owner, a reminder that it is not, could never be, just mine.

Oh shit. When's the funeral?

he says, ending the blunt by pressing it against the window-pane. A shame, seeing the smoke drift away from it like that, a death too early.

I know my Aunty's words. Forgive. Forget. But no matter how hard I try, I still remember. My mind an old VHS tape, on repeat.

Of course, everyone kept on living: Aisha went to college on a full ride, just like Noreen. She's a manager at a hotel now. Got married to a woman who's a sculptor. Noreen went to college and then graduate school, a fancy architecture job in a downtown Chicago high-rise building. These are the things about them I gathered from social media. Successful orphans. So good at hiding, no one would know. On paper, I kept living too. Graduated early. Worked for a year while I stayed in a room I found on Craigslist, another apartment of strangers. Then went to college. Scholarship kid. A camp counselor. After-school arts teacher. Scraped together money to pay rent each month. And of course, I was good at showing the world I was alive: posted the occasional photo on Facebook and Instagram, made friends in the cities I lived in, learned how to cook a few things, stopped eating Zebra Cakes for dinner. But inside, I feel frozen. All around me, quiet.

I never thought he would be gone. My Uncle ███. His body in the hallway. *You're easier to be around than your sisters.* The light swinging from above. His hands around my throat. Him watching me as I sat on the mattress, unable to move. Him checking our schedules. *Who are they going to believe?* And then, just like that, one day, suddenly he's gone, past tense. He was.

We bury people quickly. If we embalm, the body won't be able to return. So it's fast. The same day even, if we can, the next day if we can't. A day to say goodbye. A night to travel. I look at the text again. *Tomorrow.* I stare at my sister's name shining up from my phone, glistening perfect.

Noreen. God of the Texts. God of the Orphans. God of Tomorrow.

He wants to come with me, the boy with the blunt, to the funeral. It surprises me when he says it, his thoughtfulness, the idea that he might think that I need someone there and the idea that someone might be him. I can see it—what he wants: so clear it seems like a movie I could watch, a movie that I would cry about after, wondering why my life never seemed to turn out as romantic as the stories we watch onscreen. We're talking, there: in that apartment with the mismatched furniture. I'm not in my body but watching from the kitchen counter. My body is still pretending to be a girl, even though I'm not. He says he didn't know that I still talked to my sister, that Uncle ███ was still alive. *So he's the one who raised you?* he asks, trying to map a map that's mapless, a map with no legend.

My janamaz is draped over the yellow chair that one of my friends gave to me when she moved a few months ago. He touched it earlier, said that I should hang it up on the wall because it was so pretty. Idiot. I'm always surprised by how much shit you have to explain to people who aren't Muslim. I got uncomfortable when he touched it, his hand so close to my God.

He's waiting for my answer, and I wonder why I never took the time to make this apartment home. Sure, there were other apartments, a long line of them really. But I always loved the way that the light entered the living room here in the morning. I could've gotten a couch that fit better, instead of a hand-me-down, one that came with the apartment already, one that countless people had probably fucked on before I did. He says that I never talk about my childhood, that he's been trying not to press, but he wants to know. I wonder if I'll be the last person to have this couch. Where it might go after me. If this is its ending, or beginning.

What happened? With you and your sisters?

It's soft, his words, a bunny on a landmine. My lungs start to press against my ribs, a feeling I haven't felt in years, since I've been away from them, since I faded so quietly that I disappeared.

I have to go be with my family,

I say, surprised by the word. *Family*. Aisha's feet dangling off the fire escape. Noreen's laugh, lilting through the room. I haven't seen them in years.

I feel my flame spark. Around me, smoke. Around me, everything becomes desert. The scorpion stinger rises. It wants to hook into someone. After all these years. It wants to make something bleed.

I thought that's what you and I were. Family.

Family. Aisha. Noreen. Uncle ███████. Aunty. Meemoo. My dead mom. My dead dad. The apartment. The fire escape. The twin trundle. All the doors inside me lock.

There I am: in front of the apartment building, standing on the street with a bag. The doors have been repainted. Yellow, of all colors. Staring out at the street, the entrance to a zoo. Whoever repainted it probably thought that it would be inviting. From outside it looks smaller than I remember. I think they might be staying here, Aisha and Noreen. I could go inside. I bet my key still works. I could open the door, I could walk up the stairs, I could walk into our old apartment we shared with Aunty and Meemoo, with Aalia and Tiffany. I could walk downstairs to the one-bedroom and see if they're still here. They could be. But I didn't ask in the text. Just said *I'll be there*, and I am. Here. My breath a little too short. My lungs uncomfortable against my ribs. After all these years. Here.

Instead, I book a hotel for two nights nearby. A shitty one, not much, and when I get there I smash a roach crawling up the wall with my sneaker. I call to the front desk and they give me thirty dollars off. I contemplate bringing some more roaches inside and calling down some more, wondering if I could get the whole room to be free. It seems unfair, that I have to pay money to even be at this fucking funeral. I know that if I had said yes, if he had come with me, we would probably be staying somewhere nicer because he would have helped pay. But instead, he's half a country away, in his own apartment, maybe waiting for me. Maybe not. I left. He called me a few times. I didn't answer. He stopped calling. Maybe he's with someone else now. People move on so fast. And I feel so temporary. I make a list of all the things I could tell him: how I walked to my childhood parks, the yellow door, the shitty receptionist downstairs who talks to you while she's on the phone so it's hard to know who she's talking to. I wonder what it would be like if I stopped pretending to be a girl. If he'd still stick around. Maybe he'd finally let me peg him. Maybe not. But honestly, his ass-cleaning hygiene is a little sus. Nary a lota in sight. We'd have to work on that. I don't think he's gonna call back. I pull out a hotel towel and put it on the floor. My fake-ass janamaz. *Allah, please forgive me for being janky,* I say. I fold my knees.

I didn't have time to find a white kurta, so I'm in a white dress with a duputta draped around my shoulders. The dress is inappropriate for a funeral, cut low in the back so you can see the soft indent of my spine when I walk. Haraam. But hey. It's the kind of dress that I can't wear outside by myself at night because I know it'll make walking down the street hard. I can only wear it when I know I'm going to be with someone, when they shield the stares. But this is the dress that I've shown up to Uncle ████'s death day in and I've never been more confident wearing it anywhere.

When I get there, there's a few people from the neighborhood, older South Asian people who don't recognize me after all these years. And Uncle ████'s wife and the two sons. His oldest son's round face. His youngest son's narrow nose. His wife's stern eyes. Her blond hair, now white. The family he so desperately wanted to love him. They ignore me when I walk in, and I take a seat at the back. A whole city between us. A whole suburb. The PATH. A bus. Fifteen blocks. A watered, flowered lawn. A house and a trundle. I wait, trying to be patient, the sweat in my armpits gathers. Until out of the corner of my eye, I see a figure come in and settle down behind me.

Hey, little one.

———

I turn and there is Aisha: hair cropped short around her ears, wearing a long white kurta and pants, smelling like rose. Her soft round face, honey radiating off of her. My younger God, cheeks pinked with blush. Our eyes lock and mine instantly water and Aisha laughs, her smile bright, free.

Have you seen—

She doesn't need to finish the sentence, the lump in her throat swallowing the name.

The casket is open, but neither I nor Aisha has gotten up to look at Uncle ████. I've moved back to the row that she's settled down in, we're together, knee to knee, looking at her phone as she shows me pictures. Her partner is beautiful, long black hair that sweeps to mid-back, brown skin, almond eyes, pregnant. Their little apartment in New Jersey, they're painting the nursery room yellow.

Remember how you painted the bunk bed yellow and didn't even open the windows? We were high for days.

A thing I don't remember, but it feels so familiar I laugh anyway. The picture of the three of us, little balloons on no food and huffing paint, in our own orbits. I wonder how it would be if all our memories stacked up together, what would be real and what would be make-believe.

Did you go by the apartment? It's yellow. I think he painted it for you, Aisha muses, and I look at her, surprised.

He missed you a lot when you left. He always loved you the most, Aisha laughs, gently squeezing my hand. And a thought I never had before: him, in our apartment, missing me.

Are you with someone? You were always with someone.

———

I think of the person who asked to come with me here. The person I did not let come. The person I left. The person my mind keeps floating to.

I'm with you.

It comes out of my mouth before I even have time to think. Aisha's eyes glisten for a moment.

We hear a click of a heel and we both turn at the same time. And there, framed in the doorway, is Noreen.

reasons why people stay—

Noreen, in a smart white suit, white heels, straight hair falling just around her shoulders. Noreen with her thin face, with her brown eyes, looking right at us.

Should we go together? she asks, coming up to us.

And like little ducks, Aisha and I join Noreen's procession, walking up to Uncle ▓▓▓▓ together. And there he is: dead, a little blue in the face, more bloated than he was when he was alive. And suddenly, less scary. Like a stranger. Wrinkled, wearing lipstick. The pink color against his skin. Soft face. His closed eyes. An old man.

Uncle ███████, in the car, looking at something I can't quite see. His hands on the wheel. The hair on his fingers bold.

Don't let the small things become the big things.

Noreen's smile on her thin face is the same, as always. She could be in high school. She could be four. She could be in a nursing home. Aisha's rounded cheeks, the dimple by her lip. *Sisters*. The word sounds foreign. Not what we are. Not what we ever were. A small word. Trying to hold us together. Brown eyes to brown eyes to brown eyes. The slight curve of Aisha's lips, moving upwards, a smirk. *Make it last, make it last.* The light in Noreen's eyes. *Make it last, make it last.* The laugh, brewing there, just beyond her eyes. Daring one of us to break first.

Sister. Sister. Sister. Sister. Sister.
Sister. Sister. Sister. Sister. Sister.
Sister. Sister. Sister. Sister. Sister.
Sister. Sister. Sister. Sister. Sister.
Sister. Sister. Sister. Sister. Sister.
Sister. Sister. Sister. Sister. Sister.
Sister. Sister. Sister. Sister. Sister.
Sister. Sister. Sister. Sister. Sister.
Sister. Sister. Sister. Sister. Sister.
Sister. Sister. Sister. Sister. Sister.
Sister. Sister. Sister. Sister. Sister.
Sister. Sister. Sister. Sister. Sister.
Sister. Sister. Sister. Sister. Sister.
Sister. Sister. Sister. Sister. Sister.
Sister. Sister. Sister. Sister. Sister.
Sister. Sister. Sister. Sister. Sister.
Sister. Sister. Sister. Sister. Sister.
Sister. Sister. Sister. Sister. Sister.

Before we worshipped one God, we worshipped trees. Yes, there was the moon. Always, the moon. But don't forget about the trees. The banyans, their winding, weeping, walking ways. Where our ancestors live. They grow in the crevices, in the places we overlook. A single tree in a maze of branches, making a whole forest of itself, a family all on its own. Ribbons dangle from stems, blowing pink in the wind. Prayers stack on prayers, a million prayers over thousands of years, prayers that sing when you touch the bark. The trees sing to each other, across the borders, across the villages. Their constant chatter, their gupshup. They family each other. Even when a border is drawn between them. Even when one tree lies. Even when one tree wants space, a galaxy of their own. Even when a djinn takes hold of one tree's leaves. They love each other—the trees. They root down. They root towards each other. Their boughs, digging into the ground below, feeding the earth. The young replacing the old, a loop that loops forever. All the siblings, wrapped around each other. Sister branches, stealing each other's clothes. Brother branches, snuggled against the parents. The parents, annoyed and tired. Complaining about money. The fuckup Uncle, on his same fuckshit. The not-quite-brother-not-quite-sister branches, venturing outward. The elder branches, holding the frame in place, before dying off, before flowing back into the earth, before becoming something new.

ACKNOWLEDGMENTS

Thank you, Allah: Great Creator, Great Story, Great Mystery, for my life. Thank you to all my teachers. Thank you for giving me the opportunity to tell this story, this work of fiction, to remove pain from my body and yoke it into this book. Thank you for showing me there's a greater story, beyond pain and isolation.

I pray this book heals. I pray this book is a healing in my family, in my lineage, in my ancestry. I pray this is a healing in myself.

Ameen.

I started this book in isolation, when the sadness was so unbearable I couldn't remember who I was. I started writing it in secret, letting what came come. I didn't know where it was taking me. I didn't know what it was. I let it come. I continued this book in isolation. I made a mistake: I convinced myself that I could do it alone.

It's a trick of the orphaned mind to believe you were born into aloneness. That there is no escaping it. It's the trick: that you can build a home by yourself, where you won't need anyone, because then you won't lose anyone again. It keeps you there. It kept me there for too long. It crept into my mind, shadowing so that I couldn't see who was there around me, the long lines of them, the ones who had been shaping me all this time.

Nothing is done in isolation. I am not alone because they are dead. I am not alone because my life is so full with people, so full with books, so full with love and ideas that I can reach out and touch. I can't be alone when every person in my life is a galaxy, a world on a world in themselves. I can't be alone when I have never been, when they've been with me this whole time. When they make me, when they shape me, when actually it feels as though every breath I breathe and everything that I write is actually so deeply shaped by everyone around me, by the world, and by the authors who I am molded by and in conversation with.

What hope—that we exist in such interconnectedness. How silly I feel for the moments that I thought anything other than that. There's no part of me that would ever want us to detangle ourselves from each other. Because there is the reason to live. Each other. The ones who left and the ones who've stayed. Ya Allah, how lucky I am. I am so grateful for my dead. I am so grateful for my living. I am.

As Ross Gay writes in the beautiful acknowledgments of his book *Be Holding*, "This joy-ning is not without a little ambivalence sometimes in the world-destroying capitalist nightmare fantasy of the individual. Oh shit, I've never made anything by myself! Oh shit, I maybe am not a myself! Oh shit, I *definitely* am not a myself! Oh shit, it's all been given to me! It's all been given to me. Oh. O. Thank you."

So, here is a brief, and completely incomplete, accounting of the things that have been given to me, without which this book would never exist. For this book is after you all, and so many more:

Thank you to Douglas Kearney, whose bright and luminous work has always shown me how to make visual what is emotional. Thank you for the study, for the rigor, and for how lucky I feel to spend so much time reading your work.

Thank you, William Golding, for your work *Lord of the Flies*. For the boys who are stranded. For the stranding. For the book that I return to over and over, when I am stranded, to remember.

Thank you to Justin Torres. Thank you for *We the Animals*. When I read your book it gave me permission. It gave me vignettes. It gave me lyric. It hooked into my heart and made it feel as though I could write fiction, as though it could be possible for me to venture forward in my own discoveries. The best writers give permission. Thank you for your work, which permissions me.

Thank you to Paul Auster, for *City of Glass*. The Tower of Babel. Language never being enough and yet, being my whole world. Thank you for closure. For what is said and what is not.

Thank you to Haroon Khalid, for your book *In Search of Shiva: A Study of Folk Religious Practices in Pakistan*. Thank you for your book's insistence on remembering. It insists on holding what the state tries to forget. I found your book, or it found me, when I needed it most. When I felt broken & afraid. & then— your words. Your documentation. How much of a gift it is. It filled me. It made me see. It made me hope. And it helped reach me towards an ending for this book. Your chapter on sacred trees, and when you talk about the banyans, is the only reason this book could be concluded. The last section of this book is both influenced by and dedicated to you. Thank you.

Thank you to Akwaeke Emezi, for your exploration of being and spirit in *Freshwater*. Thank you for languaging all the selves. Reading your description of moments of dissociation was incredibly powerful and helped open something inside me, and carved a path for me to write about dissociation. Thank you for shining a light that bounces, and allows and allows. Thank you for the permission of that book, for the great opening it allows. And thank you for the term *brother-sisters*, which helped me so much.

Thank you to Carmen Maria Machado for *In the Dream House*. Thank you for breaking silence, and allowing so many others to do the same.

Thank you to Arundhati Roy for *The God of Small Things*. Thank you for all the Gods. Thank you for all the small things. Thank you for that book, my copy of which is so battered that all the pages are falling out.

And thank you to Khudejha Asghar and Ruquia Asghar, whose words, lives, love, and ideas have always influenced me. Thank you to my sisters for protecting me, for loving me all the beautiful ways that are so specific to us. Thank you to Aunty Kaniz and Uncle Fuzzy, whom I am eternally grateful to be loved by.

Thank you for all the language wherever I have found it. It is through you that I can try to explain my me. And I am so grateful.

Some books cut so close to the heart that you are reborn after. That you can't be the same. I don't know how this book will resonate with the world. But, this book has done that for me. Cut me open and rebirthed me.

Thank you to my guides and ancestors. Thank you to the lineages who made me and the lineages who hold me. Thank you to the lineages that are not mine but who have made space for me, who have invited me in as guest, who I have learned and continue to learn so much from. Thank you for keeping me guided and grounded. Thank you for showing me my next step. Every step of the way. Thank you for showing me my next word, my next sentence. My next move. Thank you for gently bringing me towards my truth, even when I couldn't bear to touch it.

For privacy I won't name you, but thank you to my therapist. And all my healers. Y'all are the realest. Thank you for guiding me. Thank you for all the readings. Thank you for tapping. Thank you for the help.

Thank you, Jamila Woods, for your friendship. For how at ease I feel around you. For how you've helped me with this book. I could not have written this (or, let's be real, anything) without you.

Thank you to One World, Nicole Counts, Oma Beharry, and Rachel Kim for believing in me, for supporting me, and for helping me birth this book forward. And to our little LA One World coven and our beautiful retreat—Safia Elhillo, Donovan Ramsey, and Jay Ellis.

Thank you to my cousins: Sarah, Charlotte, Sara, Farhan, Amina, Fauzia, Neelo. To all my aunts and uncles. To my niblings: Emani, Zain, Aadam. Nuala and Kiyan. Adan.

Thank you to Dark Noise, my faithful loves. How lucky I am that you are mine. That I am yours. Aaron Samuels, Franny Choi, Jamila Woods (yes! I am naming you again!), Danez

Smith, and Nate Marshall. Thank you for being my family in writing.

My other family in writing and also in faith, thank you, my dearest Mashallahs: Kaveh Akbar, Angel Nafis, Hanif Abdur-raqib, and Safia Elhillo (yes, bb, you too get named twice).

Thank you to everyone who helped me navigate the terrain of this book, who read it, who I spoke to it about, who offered me love and words of insight, who read drafts and gave notes: Krista Franklin, Franny Choi (a double name!), Randa Jarrar, Fariha Roisin, Danez Smith (yes, another double!), Perry Janes, Hieu Minh Nguyen, Chani Nicholas, Sonya Passi, Fran Tirado, Vincent Martell, Jordan Phelps, Eve Ewing, Rachel McKibbens, Hollis Wong-Wear, and Sam Sax.

To my team: Jonas Brooks, Lauren Holland, Tara Dorfman, Carter Cofield, Stephanie Smallings, Amy Nickin—thank you. Gratitude to Tabia Yapp and the whole team at Beotis: Vanity Gee, Irena Huang, Tayler Lord, and Morgan Howard. Tabia: thank you for believing in me, for always showing me my worth, and for fighting to defend that.

Thank you to Troutbeck, for letting me write. Thank you for giving me space and food. You have no idea how much of an aid it is.

And thank you to the vast terrain of people who have had their lives intersect with mine, who have taught me so many lessons, who I feel blessed to know: Teodora Kaltcheva, Marilyn Paschal, Jaspreet Kaur, Nabila Hossain, Rehan Siddiqui, Mo

Browne, Cam Awkward-Rich, Diamond Sharp, José Olivarez, Shira Erlichman, Justin Phillip Reed, Laura Brown-Lavoie, Jess Snow, Sarah Kay, Phil Kaye, Amina Sheikh, Ceci Pineda, Marco Lambooy, Jasmin Panjeta, VyVy Trinh, Dimress Dunnigan, Kush Thompson, Raych Jackson, Britteney Kapri, Zarif Wilder, Jacqui Germain, Amy Sewick, Mina Zachkary, Fawz Mirza, Laura Zak, Bisha Ali, Yolo Akili, Andria Mirza, Pidgeon Pagonis, Clint Smith, Matt Muse, and Dominique James.

To everyone else I have met, who has influenced me, and who has been there—you have my gratitude. Thank you.

PHOTO: MERCEDES ZAPATA

FATIMAH ASGHAR, author of *If They Come for Us,* is a poet, filmmaker, educator, and performer. They are the writer and co-creator of *Brown Girls,* an Emmy-nominated web series that highlights friendships between women of color. Along with Safia Elhillo, they are the editor of *Halal If You Hear Me,* an anthology that celebrates Muslim writers who are also women, queer, gender-nonconforming, and/or trans. They wrote and were a coproducer on *Ms. Marvel* for Disney+.

fatimahasghar.com
Twitter: @asgharthegrouch
Instagram: @asgharthegrouch

ABOUT THE TYPE

This book was set in Walbaum, a typeface designed
in 1810 by German punch cutter J. E. (Justus Erich)
Walbaum (1768–1839). Walbaum's type is more
French than German in appearance. Like Bodoni,
it is a classical typeface, yet its openness and slight
irregularities give it a human, romantic quality.